A School So Bad It's Criminal

PILFER ACADEMY

Lauren Magaziner

Dial Books for Young Readers

Dial Books for Young Readers
Penguin Young Readers Group
An imprint of Penguin Random House, LLC
375 Hudson Street • New York, NY 10014

Library of Congress Cataloging-in-Publication Data
Magaziner, Lauren.
Pilfer Academy : a school so bad it's criminal / Lauren Magaziner.
pages cm
Summary: "When George is brought to Pilfer Academy, a secret school for training
young thieves, he has the time of his life . . . until he realizes he's much too
good-hearted to actually steal anything"— Provided by publisher.
ISBN 978-0-8037-3919-2 (hardback)
[1. Schools—Fiction. 2. Robbers and outlaws—Fiction. 3. Conduct of life—Fiction.
4. Humorous stories.] I. Title.
PZ7.M2713Pil 2016 [Fic]—dc23 2015017309

Printed in the United States of America
1 3 5 7 9 10 8 6 4 2

Design by Nancy R. Leo-Kelly
Text set in ITC Berkeley Oldstyle

To Super Poppop and Best Bubbie—
from whom I've stolen the Gold brains
and the Antman heart

The Wrong Place at the Wrong Time

The small truck had parked two houses away from George's home so as not to arouse suspicion. But the neighbors kept looking at it, tapping their feet expectantly before getting frustrated and moving on. One toddler even banged on the side of the window and shouted, "CHIPPITCH!" until her mom dragged her away, still screaming and thrashing about.

"Are you sure this was the right vehicle?" the woman in the truck asked.

The man in the driver's seat grunted.

"We're awfully inconspicuous. Or is it conspicuous? I can never remember."

"It's spickerous," the man replied.

The woman thought for a moment. "I suppose . . . if

we tried to hide, then we'd look too much like we were trying to hide, so by not hiding, we are hiding even more than if we were hiding."

"Mmmm."

The woman adjusted her fake mustache. "Plus we have these handy disguises."

"Irreputably. We will blend in perfectly with hats, glasses, trench coats, wigs, and fake mustaches. No one will espect a thing!"

The woman laughed, and then the man laughed. It was a nice rousing burst of evil laughter that went wholly unappreciated by the teenager who happened to pass by at the moment. Then, the man and the woman cleared their throats and sobered.

They sat, the people in the van. They sat, and they sat, and they sat. Silent. Still. Patiently waiting.

George never noticed that anything was amiss.

When he woke up, hours after the van had nestled in front of the neighbor's yard, the only thing he saw was the lazy haze shining through his window. It took him five more minutes to hear the shouts coming from the other kids in the neighborhood, and another five minutes after that to notice that there wasn't a single noise in the house, an impossible occurrence with his eight-person family.

He knew he was being punished after last night, when he stole Gunther's dessert right off his plate and stuck it in his mouth before anyone could say anything about it. It was worth it, just to see the look on Gunther's face. His mom had yelled a lot, though, and called him Naughty George, which was her favorite nickname for him.

As he lay in bed in his silent house and grinned, he couldn't help but feel that being naughty had its perks sometimes—it was the first time he'd had the room to himself in ages, and he wanted to treasure the moment. It was hard to get any peace and quiet when sharing a room with Gunther. Whenever Gunther was in the room, George somehow always ended up in a headlock. There was no way to describe Gunther except meaty, and there was no way to describe their room-sharing experience except painful. George had the wrestling bruises to prove it.

He rolled out of bed and shuffled downstairs to the kitchen. His parents hadn't bothered to leave a note, but they rarely did anymore. They were the kind of parents that didn't dote on their children, and their primary goal was to make their kids as independent as possible as early as possible. George supposed it was working because he hadn't remembered the last time he felt like he really *needed* his parents to do anything for him, which made him sad but proud at the same time.

George made a three-egg omelet, fashioned himself a cup of tea, and sat down at the head of the table with his parents' newspaper, feeling very grown-up indeed. Of course, he didn't actually *read* the newspaper; it was terribly boring. He just held it and pretended. It was fun to act like his father sometimes, when no one was looking.

When George was done with breakfast, he thought that he ought to make use of an empty house, so he went right to all the places he wasn't allowed to enter, like Derek and Corman's room. Derek was about to head off to college, and Corman was going into tenth grade. They were constantly holed up in their room, and they only ever left to go to school, sports practice, and to hang out with their equally peculiar friends. His mom loved to talk about "teenage angst," "hormones," "puberty," and "growing up," but George was pretty sure that his older brothers were just plain weird.

Still, he couldn't leave them alone. They were a bizarre teenage mystery. One that George just *had* to solve.

He stood in front of their door, looking at the signs tailored specifically for him.

GO AWAY, GEORGE.

STOP STEALING OUR STUFF, SQUIRT.

GET OUT. THIS MEANS YOU, GEORGE.

DO NOT UNDER ANY CIRCUMSTANCES
    BLAST THE STEREO.

George ignored the signs, walked in, and blasted their stereo anyway.

He opened up their sock drawer, and a positively revolting stench wafted from it. He immediately closed the drawer and opened another. He rifled through, finding some paper clips, buttons, and sticks of gum. He pocketed the gum. Then he went to Corman's night table and found his comics, which he tucked under his arm to borrow and return later (maybe) when Corman was out. In Derek's night table, he found ten dollars.

George pumped his fist in the air. "Money!" he shouted over the techno-music.

He jumped on their beds, and when he finally got bored, he scurried to the other room he wasn't allowed to be in—his sisters' room. Colby, Corman's twin sister, and Rosie, the five-year-old baby of the family, shared a room that he wasn't ever allowed to enter because his mom repeatedly reminded everyone that girls needed their privacy.

But George couldn't really understand why. It wasn't like Colby's diary said anything interesting anyway— just a bunch of boring stuff about boys with little hearts in the margins. And Rosie's side of the room just had Mr. Snuggles, her favorite stuffed animal, but it was *hardly* breaking news. George cracked the door open and peeked his head inside, wondering if he'd be able to read the latest installment in Colby's non-existent love life. But the smells of lotions and the sight of pink lacy pillows were so overwhelming that he grabbed the diary to take with him.

With Corman's comics, Derek's money, and Colby's diary in hand, George slammed the door shut, scampered wildly down the hallway, and—SMACK.

He ran right into his mother, who was carrying shopping bags into her room. The comics, diary, and money flew up in the air and fell down like a hard rain.

"Uh-oh," George said.

His mother's eyes narrowed on Colby's diary and Corman's comics. "Uh-oh is *right*, young man! What are you doing with your siblings' things? I thought we taught you to respect their privacy!"

Colby bounded up the stairs. "YOU'RE READING MY

DIARY?" she shrieked when she saw it sprawled on the floor.

"It's not that interesting anyway!" George said.

"That's not the *point!*"

"QUIET!" his mother shouted, putting her hand up, just as Rosie and Gunther popped up the stairs, too. "George," she said, rubbing her temples like she had a headache coming on, "why are you *always* getting into trouble?"

"I'm not *always*—"

"I don't know what I'm going to do with you—why do you feel the need to be the naughty one in the family, George?"

"I'm not the—"

"George," his mother said sternly, "no one else causes half as much trouble as you!"

The door to the garage opened, and George could hear his two oldest brothers horsing around as they walked into the house.

His mother waggled a finger at him. "You're grounded, George."

"You can't ground me for walking around!" George said.

"You were reading *my diary!*" Colby screeched.

"Not now, Colby! Let me handle this."

"What's going on?" called George's dad from downstairs.

"George was—"

"George? Again?" shouted his father. "He was just punished yesterday!"

George gritted his teeth. He couldn't take it anymore. Before anyone could say another word, he grabbed the ten-dollar bill off the floor, slid under his mom's arms, pushed past his siblings, barreled into his dad, ran out of the house, and sprinted far, far down the street.

He walked through the neighborhood, toward the source of all the screaming kids. Every summer, the kids his age always played kickball, manhunt, capture the flag, and four square in the grassy space where everyone's backyards connected. He didn't have many friends—he was the kid in class who always caused a ruckus and left whoopee cushions on his teacher's chair, so he was revered by half the class and hated by the other half. His high jinks left him a little lonely, but he could never stop being mischievous—it was just his nature.

He trudged down the wiggly road, trying to balance on the curb.

Then came a sound.

The most marvelous, glorious sound.

The kind of sound that makes sparrows sing, hearts

dance, and grown men fall to their knees weeping with joy.

"THE ICE-CREAM TRUCK!" George shouted.

It was driving right behind him. Had it been there the whole time? He had been so distracted he didn't even notice.

He started to walk toward it, but the truck zoomed past him.

"HEY, WAIT!" he cried, sprinting as fast as he could and waving his arms wildly. The music was playing, but the truck kept speeding away.

George ran down three streets and cut across a stranger's lawn—finally catching up to the ice-cream truck. It had parked in an emergency lane just outside his neighborhood. For a fleeting second, he wondered why an ice-cream truck would stop where there were no houses around. Wouldn't it make more sense to park the truck closer to all the backyards? With all the kids playing capture the flag, the ice-cream scooper was sure to make hundreds of bucks.

But the thought passed when he walked up to the ice-cream truck and saw the menu. Did he want a Chipwich? Or a Choco Taco? Or a Fun Cone?

"I'll have an ice-cream sandwich, please," George said.

"We're not serving that today," a bony, lanky man

said. He had a deep and rumbling voice, like a rattling engine.

"Okay, I'll have a lime fruit pop, then."

"Don't have that, either." The man leaned over the counter, and George noticed he had a sharp, angular face—and a funny black mustache that looked a little too groomed to be real.

"Well, what *do* you have?"

"We got Triple-dipple Ultra-deluxe Melty Creamy Creamer Rainbow Swizzle Milk Munch ice cream."

"What else?" George asked.

"That's it," the man said.

"I've never heard of it before. How much?"

"Ten bucks."

"*TEN* bucks?" George choked. "What a rip-off!"

"Take it or leave it, kid, but it's the best ice cream on this side of the continent."

George dug into his pocket and fished out Derek's money. "Okay, fine."

"I can give you Triple-dipple Ultra-deluxe Melty Creamy Creamer Rainbow Swizzle Milk Munch ice cream on a cone, or Triple-dipple Ultra-deluxe Melty Creamy Creamer Rainbow Swizzle Milk Munch ice cream in a cup."

"Cone, please."

The man went in the back and rustled around. There came *CLANGs* and *WHUMPs* and *CRASHes* and *BAMs*. It sounded like he was building a robot, not scooping triple-dipple whatever ice cream.

At last, the man with the thin face popped up over the serving counter again. "Okay, kid, your ice cream is all ready. Just come around the back of the truck to get it."

George scurried to the back of the truck. The doors swung open, and the man stood there, his mustache askew. Except that the man wasn't a man at all—he was a *woman.*

George furrowed his eyebrows. "Hey! What are you—?"

The woman threw something that looked like a bouncy ball at him. With a *POP!* and a hiss and a flash of smoke, the ball expanded into a net that trapped George in its web. George tried to run away, but he tripped over the netting and fell on the ground.

"HELP!" he screamed. "SOMEONE HELP ME!"

The woman jumped out of the truck and plucked George off the ground with ease. He screamed and tried to bite her, but the netting was small and thick, and George ended up with a mouthful of mesh.

She pulled him all the way into the ice-cream truck and locked the door. "DRIVE!" she shouted to the man in the driver's seat—an actual man this time. George could tell from his big hulking frame, and the fact that, when he turned around, he was wearing one of those fake black mustaches over his already-prominent, golden-colored handlebar mustache.

He grunted, put his foot on the gas, and away they drove.

Navigating North

George was tossed around in the back of the van like scrambled eggs as the truck sped down the highway. The woman fastened him down with some heavy-duty duct tape. George spat at her, and he only narrowly missed her face.

"THIS IS ILLEGAL," George screamed. "THIS IS KID-NAPPING!"

"This is *not* kidnapping," the woman said. "This is a highly successful mission of person-stealing."

"I have two parents and four older siblings who are going to beat you up if you don't return me."

The woman leered at him.

"WHO ARE YOU?" George said, pushing against his bonds. "WHAT DO YOU WANT WITH ME?"

The woman ignored him and went back to navigating

the double-mustached driver. She peered at a clearly upside-down map and pulled out binoculars to look out the window. After about a half hour on the road, she made the double-mustached man stop the car.

The woman left the door wide open as she stepped out onto the side of the road. She licked her finger and held it up in the air. "The wind is blowing from all directions, which means we should head NorthWestSouthEast," she said matter-of-factly.

The man hopped outside and leaned on the van, which wobbled when he put his weight on it. "We just have to fellow the North Star," he grunted.

"Magnificent idea, Ballyrag!" They made a big show of looking high and low and left and right and up and down for the North Star.

"I'm going to check under the car," the woman said.

"STOP!" George shouted, struggling with the heavy-duty tape tying him down. "It's the middle of the after-noon."

"It *is*?" said the man named Ballyrag. "Strongarm! It's the middle of the afternoon."

"It is?"

"It is."

There was a pause. Ballyrag scratched his head.

"You know what that means?" George prompted.

"Undubiously!" Ballyrag said. "It's time for tea and rumpets with raspberry preservatives."

"Don't forget the clotted cream!" shouted the woman, Strongarm, from under the truck.

George rolled his eyes. "No, it means you won't find the North Star. The sun's still out."

"Oh." Ballyrag frowned. "Hey, Strongarm! The kid says we won't find the North Star."

"Why not?"

"The sun's still out."

"So?"

"So," said Ballyrag, "it's hiding the star."

"Well, don't worry!" Strongarm shouted, crawling out from under the car. "I'll find it, now that I know exactly where to look! If the star is behind the sun, why, then all I have to do is stare directly into the sun with my binoculars, and eventually I'll see right through it!"

"What a magniferous idea!" Ballyrag said, clapping his hands and squealing.

Strongarm held the binoculars up to her eyes and pointed them straight at the sun. Ballyrag hulked over to where George was lying, all tied up.

"I should make those rumpets, now," he said, sticking his head back in the ice-cream truck. "You know, in some countries, it's forbidden to miss teatime."

"Like where?"

"New Hampster," Ballyrag said authoritatively, twirling the ends of his golden mustache.

Unbelievable, George thought. *I've been kidnapped by idiots!*

When Ballyrag left to rejoin Strongarm in her quest to find the North Star, George realized it was the perfect time to make his escape. He wiggled and wriggled and thrashed against the tape that was gluing him to the floor of the ice-cream truck. But it was no use—he was stuck tight.

He tilted his head to see what Strongarm and Ballyrag were up to. Ballyrag was looking at Strongarm. Strongarm was still peering straight into the sun. Finally, she put down her binoculars. "See? I told you I was right. All I had to do was stare at the sun until it became nighttime. Now, quick! Someone locate the North Star!"

George tried to exchange a glance with Ballyrag, but Ballyrag was too busy scratching his head.

"It's still the middle of the afternoon," George said. "It's one of the sunniest days I've ever seen."

"So?" said Strongarm.

"So?" repeated Ballyrag.

"So you've gone blind from the sun."

"Really?" Ballyrag said. "Strongarm, are you going blinded?"

"I cannot see!" she announced. "Ballyrag! Help me!"

He walked over to her and grabbed her arm. "Where should I take you?"

"To the driver's seat!"

George spluttered. "But you can't drive if you can't see!"

"But how can I see if I can't drive?"

"Good point, good point," Ballyrag muttered.

"That is *not* a good point!" George shouted. "That doesn't make sense at all!"

After a very unsuccessful attempt of begging Ballyrag to drive, George was finally able to bribe him—his left shoe in exchange for Ballyrag in the driver's seat.

Though, why Ballyrag wanted George's left shoe was *beyond* him. Ballyrag buckled Strongarm in, then hopped in the back of the van to take what was his. He wiggled the shoe off George's foot and tied the laces around his neck to make what looked like a shoe-necklace.

Ballyrag took a big whiff and coughed. "You have stinky feet," he said as he stroked the shoe-necklace fondly. He shut the truck doors again, jumped into the driver's seat, and away they drove.

"Do you have sunscreen?" Strongarm asked Ballyrag,

after Ballyrag's third illegal U-turn. "I think my eyeballs are sunburned."

Ballyrag dug into the side compartment and found a tube for Strongarm, who globbed it on her hands and delicately swabbed her eyes.

"OWWWWWWWWW!" she howled.

George, meanwhile, was still struggling with the tape around his wrists and ankles.

They must have driven for three or four hours before the truck finally stopped. Strongarm's eyes had begun to clear up, and Ballyrag had, apparently, driven in the right direction because when Strongarm looked out the window she clapped, giggling madly. George tried to peer out the front windshield, but from where he was tied up, he couldn't see anything but a winding road that disappeared up a hill.

"We're here!" Strongarm said.

"And where's that?" George asked. "What do you want with me?"

Strongarm climbed into the back of the truck and pulled a nail clipper out of her pocket.

"Hold still," Strongarm said. "These things are *very* dangerous." She proceeded to cut the tape and netting away from him. After fifteen minutes, she succeeded.

The second his arms were loose, George pushed

her—she tumbled back and hit the wall of the truck. He jumped out its open doors, picked a direction, and ran.

But it didn't matter because Ballyrag caught up with him in less than three seconds. And no wonder—his legs were as tall as George's entire body. Ballyrag plucked George off the ground by the scruff of his shirt and dangled him as far away from himself as possible, like he was a stinky diaper. George couldn't understand this at all. He couldn't have been any stinkier than the shoe under Ballyrag's nose.

"You're running in the wrong direction," Ballyrag said. "Here." He carried George, and when they were right underneath an iron gate, Ballyrag turned him around so that he was staring at a long, twisty path that led up the hill.

And at the top of the hill was the most amazing thing George had ever seen: a beautiful Gothic manor, with taupe exterior walls and colorful stained-glass windows. The building was so wide that it looked like it had eaten seven normal-sized buildings. And all over, the mansion was adorned with striking archways and ribbed vaults and tall spires and flying buttresses. It was stunning but very out of place in the middle of nowhere, USA.

"Beautiful!" George gasped.

"We know! We splanstranted it from Europe. Here, read the graving," Ballyrag said, lowering him a bit and shoving his face in front of an engraved plaque.

PILFER ACADEMY OF FILCHING ARTS
(WE STEAL THINGS)

FINDERS KEEPERS, LOSERS WEEPERS

"TA-DA!" Strongarm and Ballyrag shouted. Strongarm even threw in some jazz hands for a TA-DA! effect.

George's mouth felt far too dry. "What is this place?" he croaked, even though he somehow knew exactly what they were going to say.

"Your new school," Strongarm said with a wicked grin, "and home sweet home."

Pilfer Academy of Filching Arts (We Steal Things)

Ballyrag carried George up the stone steps —all three hundred fifty-two and a half of them—that led into the mansion's ornate front doors.

"The entire property is locked from the outside, so no excaping," Ballyrag explained as Strongarm kneeled over to unlock the door with a key that was hanging around her neck.

She held the door open for them as they stepped into the foyer—or foy-yay as Strongarm called it. The entrance was chandelier lit, illuminating expensive Oriental rugs that covered the marble floors and ran up the symmetrical master staircases that flanked each side of the room. The two mahogany banisters were just fat enough for sliding down. More than anything, George wanted to slide right down those puppies—but as he looked around, he realized it wouldn't be possible to do that without breaking *something*.

There were ivory statues everywhere—big ones and small ones, portraying Greek gods and naked people and cupid babies. One even squirted yellow liquid out of its mouth, which George thought looked positively disgusting. Old, serious-looking paintings covered every single space on every single wall and every single column.

But there was even more—and the rest was bizarre. Right in the middle of the room, directly underneath the crystal chandelier, was the enormous skeleton of a Tyrannosaurus rex riding a World War II fighter plane. Next to it, a suit of armor was in the driver's seat of a pioneer wagon. A mummy was taunting a taxidermied bull with a red cloth. A replica caveman was typing Morse code. An astronaut suit was holding a butter churner.

It was like someone had vomited a museum right into the foyer, but hadn't bothered to fix the exhibits.

George stood in silence, utterly overwhelmed. At last, he said, "That's a very nice imitation David." He nodded toward a grand, fifteen-foot-tall stone statue somewhere along the left side of the room.

"Imitation?" Strongarm scoffed. "Imitation! I daresay, that's the *real thing*! Italy has the imitation! Everything in this academy is one hundred percent stolen."

"WOW!" Ballyrag marveled, as if he were hearing all this for the first time.

"Even the estate itself is stolen from the Duke of Valois in France—"

"He and his wife went into town for an expresso!" Ballyrag interrupted.

"And when he came back a half hour later, his manor was gone."

"Even his gardens were flinched, lawn and all!"

Strongarm gave a rousing round of applause for the ingenious theft.

George smiled halfheartedly and looked around again. "That fountain isn't part of the plumbing system, is it?" He warily eyed the ivory man who looked like he was most certainly spitting pee.

"Absolutely not!" Strongarm said, aghast. "That's lemonade!"

"Well, that's a relief," George said, even though being kidnapped by fools and trapped in a mansion full of thieves was the absolute opposite of relieving.

"Let's go to my office, Ballyrag." Strongarm scurried across the foyer, and Ballyrag stomped after her. She led them through more rooms of stately statues and stolen museum exhibits, climbing two stairways and crisscrossing the building multiple times.

"I would have introduced you to Dean Dean Deanbugle, but he's out," she said to him over her shoulder as they walked.

"Dean . . . Deanbugle?"

"Dean Dean Deanbugle," Strongarm corrected. "A Dean named Dean Deanbugle! You will meet him soon enough."

They finally stopped before a medieval oak door with decorative ironwork.

Inside, Strongarm's office was cramped and overflowing. There were cases of fancy goblets, twisty candles, wood-carved puppets, and swanky hats. There were coins of all shapes and sizes from just about every country around the globe. On the wall hung bronze pocket watches, shiny picture frames (which didn't house pictures, but instead framed smaller golden frames— frame inside frame inside frame), shimmering jewels, sparkly gems, and flashy gold nuggets. Strung around the perimeter of the room were silver chains, hanging like sparkling Christmas tinsel.

While everything that glistened was not gold, everything that glistened *was* in Strongarm's office.

"It's very . . . erm . . . shiny in here," George said.

Strongarm beamed.

"You think *this* is shiny? Just look at my Crowning Jewel!"

"Your Crowning Jewel?"

"Yes, the Crowning Jewel of my thieving career—it's thief talk for my most valuable steal!"

"So what *is* your Crowning Jewel?" George asked her.

"The Crowned Jewels!"

"Right," George said. *Of course.*

Strongarm walked over to her chest of drawers, opened the top one, and wheedled the bottom of the drawer out. "It has a fake bottom," she explained in response to George's bewildered expression. She beckoned George over to the drawer, and he peered in at a dazzling collection of jewels of all colors, shapes, and sizes.

"Those are taken right from the queen?" he asked.

"*Right* from the queen!" Strongarm confirmed.

"Snatchled from under her nose!" Ballyrag said.

"What's your Crowning Jewel?" George asked Ballyrag.

"Did you see that fancy chandelier when you first walked in?"

"Yeah?"

"Not that," said Ballyrag firmly as Strongarm dragged

29

three gem-encrusted chairs into a triangle shape and sat at one corner.

She motioned for George to sit, and so he did—only to find that it was the lumpiest, most uncomfortable chair he had ever had the misfortune of sitting in.

"Okaaaaay!" Strongarm said not a moment later, popping out of her chair. "Now that we've had a little rest and relaxation, it's time to take a tour!"

She yanked George out of his seat, pulled him back out into the hallway, and led him down a forty-foot tall corridor. Twinkling chandeliers dangled from hand-painted ceilings, and the walls were lined floor-to-ceiling with mirrors. It was like walking in his sister Rosie's ballet studio, only a thousand times grander.

"You must be blundering what all this is," Ballyrag said, gesturing widely, "here at Pilfer Academy."

George looked around. "And where is Mr. or Mrs. Pilfer?"

"Who?"

"Pilfer Academy. Is Pilfer someone's name?"

Strongarm snickered. "No, silly! Pilfer isn't a name—pilfer means *to steal*. It's just a fancy word for thievery." She cleared her throat. "Pilfer Academy of Filching Arts is the finest school for cultivating thieves, robbers, muggers, burglars, crooks, and otherwise intolerable hoodlums."

George frowned. He wasn't a thief, robber, mugger, burglar, crook, or otherwise intolerable hoodlum. Sure, he *borrowed* Corman's comics, but he was going to return them . . . maybe. And yes, he pocketed Derek's money, but it was only ten dollars. He would have paid him back, probably. He hardly thought any of that qualified him to be enrolled in a thieving school.

He opened his mouth to protest, but Strongarm plowed on. "You should be very proud of yourself," she said, trudging down a flight of stairs. "You popped up on our radar last year. Our recruitment field scouts thought you had excellent thief potential, and we've been dogging you for a while now, watching your every move—"

"—waiting to see if you'd inhibit thief qualities," Ballyrag interrupted.

"And did I?"

They both stopped walking and nodded vigorously.

"Multiple counts of thievery, general sneakiness, excellent timing, sharp intuitions, persistence, cunning, and a disregard for universal morality," Strongarm said, ticking off his offenses with her fingers.

George furrowed his brow. "So . . . what does that mean?"

"It means that you are well on your way to becoming

31

one of the top thieves in the country—no, the world."

The corridor forked at the end, and Ballyrag pointed to the left. "That's the way to the lie berry."

"The what?" said George.

"The Bonnie 'N' Clyde Lie Berry," Ballyrag said, leading him over to the stained-glass double doors that led inside. "Run by our splunderful liberrian, Bagsnatcher."

Strongarm unlocked the door with a small key hanging around her neck, then opened the doors wide. George marveled at the sight. The library was four stories tall with ladders to climb to the next level, and bookshelves that wrapped all the way around the room.

"Our library only stocks first-edition original copies, stolen directly from each author," Strongarm said proudly.

"So when people borrow books—"

"You want to borrow a book from the library?" Strongarm laughed incredulously. "You *can't* do that! We keep all the books chained to the wall to prevent that sort of thing."

"The books are *chained* to the *walls*? What use is that? The whole point of a library is to let someone take a book with them!"

Strongarm snorted. "How ridiculous! Why, if we let you borrow the books, you might never return them!"

And she strode off to show George a room filled with exotic—and mostly rotten—food.

George followed Strongarm and Ballyrag around what felt like hundreds of corridors. He had the distinct feeling that they were wandering around in circles, but they never passed the same exhibit twice.

"So what do you do here?" George asked. "Just train thieves and let them loose on the world?" They had wandered into the Butch Cassidy Wing, through a room that housed a large collection of exotic creepy crawlies. George shuddered as some sort of multicolored millipede flittered down the side of a terrarium.

Strongarm nodded and smiled widely. "That's *exactly* what we do." Then she led George through an archway into a room full of space rocks. George paused for a moment to read the plaque:

From the private collection of Neil Armstrong,
1969 moon expedition, stolen by Golddigger,
Class of 1972, for his thesis project.

Everything seemed to have a plaque on it, detailing who stole the object, from where, and when.

"Where is everyone?" George asked. "All the students, I mean."

"In their dorms. It's past curfew, but you'll meet them

soon," said Strongarm, now ushering George into a hall of gemstones and gold.

"How—how many kids have you kidnapped for this?"

"Currently, we have seventy-four students in the whole school."

Ballyrag jeered at George, his face illuminated in the glow of three different gemstones. "We could have more, though. If we wanted. We have a rolling addition policy."

"That's rolling *admission*, Ballyrag dear," Strongarm corrected in a sugary voice as they walked into a large and echoing grand ballroom. "It means that students are admitted whenever we want. We bump people up to the next grade whenever we feel like they're ready . . . which could be anywhere between six months and five years, depending on how they perform."

"*Five years?*"

"Maybe longer, maybe shorter. Then you'll become a second year, until we deem you ready to become a third year. And a third year until you are a fourth year. And a fourth year until you graduate and become a professional thief. If you add it all up, you will graduate Pilfer Academy of Filching Arts between three and twenty years from now."

"Twenty! Years!" George choked.

"According to Pilfer records, our oldest graduate of all-time was thirty-three years old."

George suddenly felt very dizzy.

"Are you all right? You're looking awfully beaky," Ballyrag grumbled.

"I—I—" he stuttered. "I can go home for summer break, right?"

"Summer what now?"

George staggered into a very green, plant-filled room, and he collapsed into a plush chair. The room had full-length windows that overlooked Pilfer Academy's botanical gardens—but George couldn't even enjoy the view. His stomach flopped, a cold sweat dribbled down the back of his neck, and everything inside his head was shouting *PANIC!*

"But what about my family? They'll be looking for me . . ."

"Oh, don't worry about them. Your parents have been sent this beautiful letter." She dug deep into her pocket and handed George a scrunched-up scroll of parchment:

Dear Parent:

   Congratulations! Your son/daughter has been accepted to the Champeaux Institute for the Extraordinarily Gifted and Talented Future Leaders of the World (CIFTEGATFLOTW for short). This is an extremely advanced, secret school, and your child has been selected to join our ranks for the next several years with a FULL PAID SCHOLARSHIP in the hopes that he/she will one day become president of the world.

Sincerely yours,
Sir William Mortimer Archibald
Samuel Washington Beauregard
Oliphant the Third

"Champeaux Institute?"

"That's pronounced Shampoo!" Strongarm said brightly.

George shook his head. "*No one* will ever believe that letter."

"They will if it's sent from Sir William Mortimer Archibald Samuel Washington Beauregard Oliphant the Third! Anyone will believe anything from someone with seven names."

"But isn't it suspicious that I just ran off to school without packing up any of my stuff? In the middle of the summer? Without saying good-bye?"

36

"We've never had a complaint yet. Of course, our address is completely secret, so there would be nowhere to send complaints. . . ."

"Telephone? E-mail? Cell?"

"No phones, no computers, no service."

George looked over at Ballyrag, who seemed to be extremely taken with his bellybutton.

"So what if my parents want me back?"

"Want you back? With a full-paid scholarship to the *Champeaux Institute for the Extraordinarily Gifted and Talented Future Leaders of the World*? You must be joking!"

His chest tightened. He wasn't even *that* fond of home, but suddenly, more than anything, he ached for Gunther's headlocks, Colby's bossiness, Rosie's whining, and Derek's and Corman's scowls every time he asked to join in on their fun. He missed his mom and dad. He even missed being labeled the Naughty One.

His anger at his parents from the afternoon suddenly seemed faded and distant. He could be trapped here for up to *twenty years*. Forced to attend school until he was— quite possibly—*thirty-three*. It could be *decades* before he saw his family again. With a rattled breath, George leaned forward and buried his head in his hands. *What do I do?* he thought. His eyes burned, and his throat suddenly felt very lumpy.

"There, there, don't worry, I'm sure you will do extraordinarily well at Pilfer," Strongarm said, completely misunderstanding.

Ballyrag came over and awkwardly patted George's elbow. "Just think, one day you will be a scream de la scream criminal—"

"Just like our most famous alums," Strongarm interrupted, "Dominic Sneakthief, Patricia Roughshock, Felicity Headlock, Sir Nicolas Hurtsalot—"

"N-never heard of them."

Strongarm rolled her eyes. "Of *course* you haven't heard of them—they've never been caught!"

Ballyrag smacked his hand against his forehead, as if to say, *obviously*!

"Come, come!" Strongarm pulled him up from the chair. "We still haven't seen the Autolycus Wing, the Ma Barker Wing, *or* the Blackbeard Wing."

George's heart was hammering as he followed Strongarm and Ballyrag through more wings of the mansion. It was confusing and overwhelming; there were so many exhibits and stolen artifacts that he felt almost dizzy.

Then they climbed to the very top of the school to look at three different observatories—stolen from different science labs around the country—and through the largest telescope, Strongarm showed him a breathtaking moonlit view of the valley town in the distance. Then they trudged down a grand staircase, and George turned right at the bottom.

Strongarm blathered on about famous alums and the prestige of the school as George followed the twisting hallways.

"Wait!" Strongarm said suddenly, interrupting herself. "We can't go down there. It's a dead end."

"A dead end?"

George peeked around the corner. The area was run-down and dark, and the only door had a sign that read:

CLEANING SUPPLIES AND VEGETABLE STORAGE
(ESPECIALLY ASPARAGUS)

Blech! George thought. Cleaning supplies and vegetables. The two worst things in the world.

"There's really nothing down here," Strongarm continued. "Come on back—let me escort you to our corridor of butter sculptures."

Strongarm showed him the Mountain of Margarine, the Butter Boat, and even the Cream-Cheese Trees—it was the weirdest room George had seen yet. And it smelled very sour, too.

Just when George thought he couldn't take one more breath, Strongarm steered him to a door that led to the back courtyard and botanical gardens. It was too dark to really appreciate the courtyard, but in the lamplight, George could see a series of stone sculptures, a hedge maze, and a spitting fountain. But the scenery was spoiled by a giant wall, twenty feet tall and extremely thick, that surrounded the grounds.

George stepped outside, into the crisp summer night. "Hey, what's that?" he asked, pointing to what looked like metal vents on the exterior wall of the school.

"It's a design feature of the school. Just think of it as a last resort," Strongarm said.

"Last resort?"

Strongarm waved her hand dismissively. "Hopefully you will never have to see it in action. Believe me, it's nothing you need to worry about."

His feet were aching and sore before too long, and his head was spinning. There were more wings and rooms than he ever would have imagined, and it would be a wonder not to get completely and totally lost. In fact, the more Strongarm and Ballyrag took him around, the more he felt like he was wandering a labyrinth of fancy halls that he'd never figure out.

"Of course, you'll recognize this," Strongarm said, leading George into a warm, gold-glistening room with a velvet carpet.

"What's this again?"

Strongarm sighed impatiently. "We saw this an hour ago. The Jesse James Wing. Your dorm." She knocked twice on the handsome bronze door and shouted, "Send me Tabitha Crawford!"

There was a scuffling of shoes and a flurry of footsteps, and the lock on the door jiggled.

But George was hardly paying attention to that. He had something on his mind, something that had been irking him from the very moment he stepped foot in Pilfer Academy of Filching Arts.

"Did you *have to* kidnap me?" he blurted out. "Why couldn't you have just *invited* me to this school?"

Strongarm sniffed. "What kind of thieving school would we be if we didn't steal our students?"

Orientation?

The door swung open. A girl with dark skin, darker hair, and even darker eyes stood in the doorway, folding her arms and looking extraordinarily grim.

The girl—Tabitha—gave George a once-over, glaring at him from head to toe. Her gaze stopped at his feet. "You know you're missing a shoe, right?" she said.

"I know," George said irritably. He was still feeling cranky and despairing and furious and miserable and dreadfully overwhelmed.

Tabitha looked at Strongarm. "Is this the new kid?"

Suddenly Strongarm gave him a forceful push, and George went tumbling forward. "See-ya-wouldn't-wanna-be-ya!" Strongarm cried, and she and Ballyrag ran down the hall, giggling wildly like a pack of hyenas.

Tabitha sighed. She pulled George through the door,

and he stepped into a large entryway with velvet couches, crowded with kids of all different ages sitting around, chatting. At the other end of the room, a spiral staircase led upward, and Tabitha dragged him toward it.

"Come on," she said. She walked quickly, and George practically had to run to keep up with her. "I'll show you the penthouse."

"The *penthouse?*"

"All the first years sleep in the penthouse. The whole dorm is four stories tall, a floor for each year. Unfortunately, first years get the top floor, which is sixty-four stairs, total. I've counted." She stopped in the middle of a step and turned around to face him. He almost crashed right into her. "Let's break here for a second."

She plopped down in the middle of the stairs.

"Uh, okay," George said.

"Okay, so welcome, welcome, and all that. I'm your 'buddy,' so if you have any questions about procedure or your schedule, just talk to me—"

"Why can't I talk to Strongarm or Ballyrag?"

"Because they have better things to do."

"Like what?" George snorted. "Learning how to pronounce words correctly?"

Tabitha rolled her eyes, but George thought he detected a little smile at the corner of her mouth. "It might not seem like it, but they really do know a lot about thieving. Like I was *saying*, whenever a new student comes, it's the old new student's responsibility to get the new new student acclimated. I arrived in May, so I've got three months of knowledge to give you."

"So you didn't have a summer break at all? That stinks."

Tabitha raised an eyebrow. "Who needs a summer break when you can be at school?"

He couldn't tell whether or not she was being sarcastic.

"C'mon, let's keep going," she said, standing up suddenly. She jumped two steps at a time, and George struggled to keep up.

She chattered on and on about the after-school clubs that Pilfer offered, like the Disguise Club, Criminal Masterminds Club, and Advanced Technology Club—but George's mind began to wander. He wondered if the stairs would *ever* end and why no one had thought to steal an elevator for the penthouse. His legs burned and ached, and he was starting to feel out of breath.

At the top of the spiral staircase, four floors up, Tabitha pointed to a left-hand door that led into a stately room with at *least* a twelve-foot ceiling, a fireplace, wall moldings, and fancy green drapes—it looked like a room for a prince. Or two princes, since there were two beds against opposite walls. A boy with a pale square face, a row of freckles, and a buzz cut was lying on one of them, holding a book straight up in front of him. The book was old, dusty, and had a broken chain attached to the spine.

"Hey," George said.

"Your bed's over there," the boy answered curtly, not even looking away from his book.

"That's Milo Hubervick," Tabitha said, scrunching her nose.

George walked over to his bed, and looked up—his last name, Beckett, was etched into a golden plaque on the wall above it.

"Great," George said awkwardly. "So, I guess we're roommates."

"Obviously."

"Right . . . so maybe we should set some ground rules?"

"Here's a ground rule for you," Milo sneered. "Just stay out of my way. I am the best in this school, and I won't have you messing me up."

Tabitha snickered. "You're kidding me, right? Let's not forget who in this room is ranked number one, and who is ranked number five."

Milo scowled at her. "You just wait until—"

"Come on, George! Follow me," she interrupted,

turning so fast that her braids whipped behind her with a whooshing noise.

George followed Tabitha across the hall to her door, and when she brought him inside, his jaw dropped. It was even *nicer* than his room, if that were possible, with gold everywhere, lace draperies, two fireplaces, a bookshelf, a rocking chair, and an enormous walk-in closet—which was like another room entirely.

"Wow!" George said.

"I know." Tabitha waved her hand, like she was unimpressed by all the nice stuff. She walked over to the bed engraved *Crawford* and rifled around underneath it until she held up a stack of crusty-looking papers. "Okay, got it! Now let's go."

"Go? Where?"

"I'm going to show you the best place in the whole dorm." She walked out, and George had to run to catch up.

Tabitha headed to a lonely door at the end of the hall and kicked it open. They scrambled up another spiral staircase and popped through another door at the top landing.

George gasped. They were on the roof, in a beautiful garden terrace. The flowers seemed to wink in the moonlight, and the formidable hill that Pilfer Academy of Filching Arts sat on cast an enormous shadow on the valley below.

He sat down on a bench next to Tabitha, and she handed over the papers, which included his schedule, a clearly unopened pamphlet of rules, and a first-year syllabus.

"Thanks!"

She frowned, studying him again with that calculating gaze of hers.

George awkwardly looked away. He opened the pamphlet to keep his mind off the fact that Tabitha was staring at him the way a lion stares at a gazelle.

He thumbed to a page in the middle.

Rule #24

Thieving of any sort will not be tolerated.

"What?" George said, examining the rule again. That seemed like the *opposite* of what the school was trying to teach. "Why?"

"Why what?" Tabitha said.

"Why won't thieving be tolerated in a thieving school?"

Tabitha shrugged. "I don't know. I don't make the rules."

"Well that one seems . . . ridiculous."

"Well, *I've* found that anything goes, as long as you don't get caught."

"That sure sounds like a great way to get the new kid in trouble," George grumbled.

She puffed up. "You really think I would do that?"

"I didn't mean it like—"

But Tabitha turned on her heels in a huff, slamming the door behind her.

Great, he thought bitterly. *Now I'm all alone.*

He leaned on the balcony and looked down into the valley. There was so much space there, but he couldn't explore any of it. From now on, he was confined to a mansion, stuck learning from a group of the nitwittiest adults he had ever encountered, and trapped with terrible, nasty thieves.

He stayed up on the roof for much longer than he should have, but at least up there, no one could hear him cry.

Quite a First Impression

George woke up the next morning feeling like he'd swallowed a bucketful of wriggling worms. It was his first day of class, but everyone else was already in the middle of the marking period. Midterms were coming up in just a month, according to his schedule, which he had read repeatedly in the glow of a flashlight before he went to bed.

He pulled it off his nightstand and glanced at it yet again:

First-Year Timetable:

6:45 a.m. to 8:15 a.m.	*Breakfast is served**
8:30 a.m. to 9:45 a.m.	*Thieving Theory (Room: Blackbeard 204) Taught by Ballyrag*

10:00 a.m. to 11:15 a.m.	Stealth 101 (Room: Butch Cassidy 347) Taught by Browbeat
11:30 a.m. to 12:45 p.m.	Lunch is served*
1:00 p.m. to 2:15 p.m.	Practical Applications of Breaking and Entering (Room: Jesse James 151) Taught by Strongarm
2:30 p.m. to 3:45 p.m.	Intro to Gadgetry (Room: Blackbeard 206) Taught by Pickapocket
4:00 p.m.	Optional snack time in the dining hall
4:00 p.m. to 9:00 p.m.	Free period
6:00 p.m. to 8:00 p.m.	Dinner is served*
8:45 p.m.	Library closes
9:00 p.m.	Curfew (until 6:00 a.m. tomorrow)

*Mealtimes can be taken within this window. Come and go as you please.

Midterms: September 15th and March 15th, 10:00 p.m.

Final Exams: June 15th and December 15th, 10:00 p.m.

Mischief Night: October 30th (No curfew)

Reminder: Absence from class will be met with <u>severe</u> <u>punish-</u>
<u>ment</u> ☹ ☹ unless you have a note from Nurse Embezzle in the
infirmary.

George folded the wrinkled paper back up again and
stuck it in his pocket. It already seemed like there was a
lot to memorize, and he hadn't even started classes yet.
He had, of course, been thinking about skipping class in
favor of looking for an escape route—until he saw the
words *severe punishment,* which was underlined several
times and had two frowny faces. He gulped, wondering
what *severe punishment* frowny-face frowny-face could
possibly mean in a school with no scruples.

He rolled out of bed and walked over to his chest
of drawers, where he found stacks of collared shirts,
sweaters, vests, nice slacks, many different colored and
patterned ties, sweatpants, gym shorts, T-shirts, sweat-
shirts, underwear, socks, and one pair of jeans. He also
found a drawer full of toiletries marked with his ini-
tials: GB.

As he put on slacks, a shirt, and a pair of Converse

51

sneakers, he was pleasantly surprised by how perfectly everything fit him. How long had they been planning for his arrival?

He walked outside to find the corridor and stairs empty—but the entrance room was full of voices.

"Come on, Robin!"

"You can do it!"

"Hold your breath!"

"No, *don't* hold your breath!"

"Thirty more seconds!"

George wandered into the room. There was a girl lying upside-down on a couch, her feet straight up in the air, her black hair almost brushing the ground. Two round-faced twin girls were cheering on either side of the upside-down girl, and a tall boy held a stopwatch.

"Uh . . . are you all right?" George said to the upside-down girl.

"Oh, I'm fine," the girl said.

"What . . . what are you doing?"

She raised an eyebrow—or lowered it, depending on perspective. "You're the new kid, right?"

George nodded.

"New kid! No way!" one of the twins said, clapping him on the shoulder. "We're all first years, too!"

The upside-down girl flipped herself off the couch and stood up, grinning. She was freckly and tiny. She ruffled her hair, which was full of uncontrollable cork-screw curls.

"Last week, we had a Practical Applications exam where we had to walk on the ceiling with sucker shoes. I passed out because of a head rush, so I'm trying to train myself—don't worry," she said, catching sight of George's nervous expression, "I was fine. They got me down eventually."

"Oh . . . okay."

"Aw, Robin! You scared him! Don't be nervous," the tall boy said, patting George on the back. "You're going to love it here! I'm Neal."

"That's Beth," said one twin, pointing to the other.

"And this is Becca," said the second twin, gesturing at her sister.

"And I'm Robin," said the curly-haired girl.

"I'm George."

"Come to breakfast with us!" Beth insisted.

After his encounters with Tabitha and Milo last night, George didn't think that his other classmates would be so friendly. But here they were, inviting him to break-fast! He could definitely use some friends. "Breakfast . . . yeah, sure!" he said.

They walked through hall after hall, and when they passed the foyer, Robin stopped for a minute to refill her water bottle with lemonade from the spitting fountain. She drank the whole bottle, filled it up again, and drank it all again. On her third refill, she smiled at George. "I can never have enough liquid sugar," she said.

"It's true," Neal said, throwing his hands up. "Robin has a crazy sweet tooth! There was this one time where she stuffed seven doughnuts in her mouth to distract a security guard while the rest of our team snuck past. Do you remember that, guys?"

Becca burst into laughter. "That was *hilarious*! The look on his face—and remember what happened—"

"When he—"

"Then they—"

"After I—"

"Yes!"

"That was soooooooo funny!"

They all looked at George, who had no clue what they were talking about.

"Uh . . . I guess you had to be there," Beth said.

George followed silently as they dragged him into the Autolycus Wing. They popped into a room full of taxidermied animals and mounted animal heads, and George walked headfirst into a dead wildebeest.

"UGH!" George said, jumping backward. "What *is* this stuff? And why is it here?"

"They're species from all across the globe—all sorts of stuffed endangered animals that were being sold on the black market," said Neal.

"These were bought on the *black market*?" George gasped. He didn't even know there *was* a black market.

"They weren't bought, George." Robin laughed. "They were stolen . . . *duh*. Thieves never buy what they can take."

"Oh, right," George said, kneeling down to stare at a stuffed sloth. Its soulless glass eyes were the absolute creepiest things George had ever seen.

They passed through more rooms of stately furniture, a room full of wooden rocking chairs and wooden clocks and wooden puppets, and a room filled with mattresses from every single president of the United States. There was no walking space, and they had to trampoline on the mattresses to get across, careful to avoid a snoring teenager curled up on one, looking like she'd fallen asleep on the way to breakfast.

The tall golden doors at the end of the mattress room opened up into the beautiful dining hall. George gaped at the arched ceilings, round tables, and a balcony that overlooked it all. A buffet line hugged the room on both sides, covered with trays and trays of food—buttermilk pancakes, wheat toast, white toast, rye toast, French toast, crepes, croissants, scrambled eggs, ten different types of omelets, eggs over easy, eggs over medium, eggs over hard, corned beef hash, home fries, hash browns, bacon strips, sausage links, scones, biscuits, English muffins, pumpkin muffins, chocolate chip muffins, bran muffins, blueberry muffins, blueberries, bananas, strawberries, raspberries, whipped cream, clotted cream, jams, jellies, chocolate sauce, caramel sauce, tea, sugar, and honey.

George's mouth watered at the sight of it all.

He copied Robin, Neal, Beth, and Becca as they each grabbed a tray and proceeded to the left buffet line, plopping scoops full of everything on their plates. When George finally got to the end, he had a mountain of breakfast food almost too heavy to carry. But he some-how managed to wobble over to the circular table where his new friends were waving him over.

As soon as he sat down, George scooped a bite of pan-cake into his mouth and felt his taste buds dance a jig. "Ist foo ist so ee-ish-us!" George hummed. He meant to say *this food is so delicious*, but with a mouthful of food, it was the best he could manage.

"Obviously," Neal said cheerfully.

George swallowed his bite. "Why obviously?"

"All the food is stolen from the finest five-star gourmet

restaurants. Only the best for Pilfer students!" Neal said with a proud nod.

"George," Beth said. She seemed to be studying him in the same way that Tabitha had yesterday. "Why are you here?"

"Um . . . I was kidnapped."

They all laughed.

"Yes, but *why?*" Robin said. "Why you? What's your talent?"

"Like, I was invited here because of my jittery fingers," Neal said. He held up his hand, and true to his word, his fingers twitched relentlessly. Even Neal himself was twitchy—he could hardly sit still without fidgeting around. "I can five-finger discount like no one's business," he bragged. "In fact . . ." He dug into his pocket, revealing four sets of utensils—George's, Robin's, Beth's, and Becca's.

They all clapped wildly.

"We're double legacy," Beth and Becca said together.

"You mean your parents are criminals?" George asked.

"Well, they're reformed now," Beth said casually, cutting into her sausage with a knife and fork. "They didn't want us to go here."

Becca nodded. "Our dad always warned us about staying away from ice-cream trucks, but . . ."

"Who can resist the call of ice cream?" Beth finished. "We went out for a walk two and a half years ago and never came back. I feel bad about that sometimes. Our parents must be so worried."

"I miss our parents," Becca said, mid-chew.

"Now, what about you?" Neal said, pointing to George. "What brought you here?"

"I—well—Strongarm said something to me yesterday . . . about cunning and sneakiness and a disregard for . . . something. I don't remember exactly."

"Well, *I* got invited because of my name," Robin boasted.

George's forehead furrowed. "Robin?"

"Robin Gold."

They all watched George carefully for a reaction.

"Robin Gold? That's not real," George finally said.

"I swear!"

"I *still* can't get over it," Neal said with a laugh.

"My parents didn't even realize until it was years too late," Robin said. "In any case, I won't have to change my name when I graduate."

"Change your name?" George asked.

"Come on. You didn't really think that Ballyrag, Strongarm, and Browbeat are their real names, did you? When we graduate, we get to choose a more intimidating name."

George laughed, thinking that Strongarm and Bal-lyrag were the least intimidating people he had ever met. "What are their real names then?" he asked, div-ing in for another bite of hash browns, but his fork hit the table. "HEY!" he said, standing up. "My plate is gone!"

He looked around. A row of teens and adults were snatching plates out from unsuspecting students. They all wore the same uniforms—burgundy blazers, stiff-collared shirts, bow ties, handkerchiefs, and scowls. George leaned in closer to see a crest emblazoned on the uniform jackets—a clawed hand grasping rubies, diamonds, and other gems. The cursive beneath the logo read *Pilfer Academy of Filching Arts*.

"The waitstaff," Becca whispered, "are the people who flunk out of the program."

George paled. *Flunk* out of the program?

An unhappy-looking pimply boy dove for Robin's plate, but she swiped it away at the last second.

"I'm not done yet," Robin said coolly.

The teenager stomped off to a different table.

"Can I get seconds?" George said. "I'm still hungry."

"Seconds?" Beth laughed. "George, you can have hun-dreds, if you really want it!"

George smiled and walked toward those beautiful

buttermilk pancakes. But as he passed Milo's table, he slowed down.

"—I don't know," Milo was whispering to a group of boys. "He arrived yesterday."

"And? How do you think he's going to rank?"

"Dunno," Milo said, leaning forward, so he was half off his chair. "But I'm not going to stand by and let some new kid steal all the attention. We have to mess with him."

"Yeah!" two boys said heartily.

"This is *our* school. And tonight let's make sure George Beckett knows his place."

George stood by the buffet, staring at the oatmeal, his heart pounding. He hadn't said two words to Milo, but already Milo was planning to sabotage him. Milo hated him, and he didn't even know why.

Anger swelled inside of George. As if being kidnapped and taken far away from his family wasn't enough. He was stuck in this stupid school, where he definitely didn't want to be. Tabitha had stormed off and left him alone last night. And to top it all off, Milo and his friends were planning something horrible. George's cheeks and ears flushed crimson, and his hands were shaking.

Before he even knew what he was doing, George

dipped a piece of toast in syrup and walked casually toward Milo's chair. Milo was leaning forward to whisper with his friends, his butt waggling in the air. Unnoticed, George slipped the toast on the seat of Milo's chair and continued walking like nothing had happened.

He briskly trotted back to his table, but as he was sitting down, he locked eyes with Tabitha, who was sitting alone across the hall. She looked at him with a wide-eyed, slack-mouthed stare. Instantly, he knew that she knew. He slowly sat down at his table.

"So, how long have you guys been here?" George asked, ignoring the fact that Tabitha was still staring at him.

"Eight months," Robin said. "I came right after the final exam in December. They passed two people on to year two, so they took Tosh Gupta and me at the same time to fill the empty slots. . . ."

George was barely listening. He kept straining to hear the inevitable sound of Milo sitting on sticky toast.

". . . and I came just over a year ago," Neal said. "Feels like forever."

"Want to talk about forever?" Beth said. "Becca and I would be starting seventh grade right now. Two and a half years of being in year one, and you'd think they'd have—"

SQUISH.

It was quiet, but George heard it.

A moment later, Milo threw a chair across the room and jumped up, looking murderous. "WHO DID THIS?"

The whole dining hall went silent. Milo peeled away the piece of French toast, but the syrup still stuck to his bottom.

"I SAID WHO DID THIS?" Milo curled and uncurled his fists like he was about to punch the nearest thing that moved.

George looked at Tabitha in panic. Was she going to tattle on him? But she just folded her arms and pressed her lips together.

"What's going on here?" asked a man holding a tray of tortellini, which George thought was the oddest choice of breakfast food.

The whole dining hall hushed as the man sauntered toward Milo.

"Sir," said Milo, bowing his head. "Someone put syrupy toast on my chair . . . and I sat in it."

"How very dastardly, indeed."

George inspected this strange man. He had eyebrows, eyebrows, *eyebrows*. It was the only thing George could think when he looked at him. They were thick and long and every-which direction, and George just wanted to comb them smooth. Beneath his eyebrows, he had a wobbly face the shape of a rotten pear with a sharp, beaky nose.

He was also bald. Completely bald, as if his eyebrows had slurped up every bit of hair from the rest of his head.

The man peered around the dining hall, and his squinted glance rested upon George. "And you are?"

"Eyebrows," George accidentally said aloud. "I—I mean George. George Beckett."

"The new boy, yes?"

George just nodded. He couldn't trust himself not to say eyebrows again.

The man inched closer, hunching over Milo like a question mark.

"I hope you weren't about to fight, Mr. Hubervick," the man said. "We are *thieves*, not thugs."

George didn't quite know the difference between a thief and a thug, but it seemed to make sense to Milo, who nodded vigorously.

"Very well," said the man, a slight frown curling at the corner of his lips. "Now . . . Mr. Beckett," the man said sternly, "could I steal a moment of your time?"

"*Me?*" George said.

"Yes, you. Follow me." The man led the way, and students parted for him as he brushed past, with George marching behind. A few people shook their heads sadly at him, and others looked worried.

"Come now," the man said, guiding George back into the room of springy president mattresses.

By the power of deduction, George knew *exactly* who the man was, why students bowed their heads when in his presence, why the whole dining hall fell hush, why following him out of the room felt like walking the plank. It didn't take a genius to figure out who could have everyone's knickers in a twist.

"Dean Deanbugle," George said, dodging a run-in with a china cabinet.

"Please," he said, holding the door to the next room open, "call me Dean Dean Deanbugle."

In uncomfortable silence, George followed the dean across Pilfer Academy—up stairs, around a loop, down stairs, and up another flight again. Around a corner, under a curtain, through a heavy bronze door, and into a musty old room with just a simple bookshelf. The dean began to push books in and pull some out in rapid succession—so fast that George almost couldn't keep up.

When he finally pushed in a yellow book, the wall rumbled and the ground started to spin. Dean Dean Deanbugle pulled George onto a rotating platform, just as the bookshelf swiveled around to the other side of the wall. George realized that the books were some sort of secret code to get into the dean's office.

The other side revealed a room with wall-to-ceiling windows, and George could see miles and miles down the hill. Far away, there were a slew of trees that stretched out like a canopy.

George moved to the window to get a better look, and the light shone in so brightly and hotly that he felt like he was under a magnifying glass.

Dean Dean Deanbugle cleared his throat, and George remembered the trouble he was in. He took a seat in the stuffy chair across from the dean's desk.

The dean leaned forward. "Let's talk about breakfast, George," he said. "I know what you did to Milo."

George's stomach dropped. He was caught. In trouble. Probably about to find out what *severe punishment* actually meant. But—in his wildest hopes—he dared to dream that they'd send him home. He didn't know whether to be terrified or excited, and he wrung his hands together anxiously.

"I'm sorry!" he finally spluttered. "I'm really really sor—"

"You may be worried that I will send you to the whirly-blerg."

"The . . . the what?" George said.

65

"The whirlyblerg. THE WHIRLYBLERG! Chamber of doom and destruction!"

George frowned.

"But I know exactly what you were doing, having once been a student myself." Dean Dean Deanbugle suddenly broke into a crooked grin. "You were trying to catch my attention! You were trying to impress me!"

"I was?"

"And I must say, I was *very* impressed."

"You were?"

"Absolutely, m'boy!"

"So you're not going to punish me?"

"Punish you? For that grand display of unparalleled stealth? For your indubitable cunning? You have exhibited amazing thief qualities, and I couldn't be prouder!"

"Oh . . . okay." George breathed a sigh of relief.

"And you didn't even say thank you! You are well on your way to becoming a hardened criminal, I see! I am very proud. Very proud, indeed!" Dean Dean Deanbugle rocked back in his chair, looking rather triumphant.

George wasn't really sure what had just happened. One minute he was about to get in trouble, and the next minute he was being patted on the back. It was all very confusing. He nodded and tried his best to look like the hoodlum Dean Dean Deanbugle wanted him to be.

"Well, you'd best be on your way to class," Dean Dean Deanbugle said. "I don't want you to be too late for . . ." he swiped the schedule out of George's hands. "Ah, yes— Thieving Theory. I just wanted to let you know that I've got my eye on you, boy. Yes, I expect great things from you."

The Key

George arrived five minutes late to his first class, which was pretty good considering he got lost in the mansion about fifteen times.

His schedule read that his class was in the Blackbeard Wing, but he couldn't remember where that was. George finally asked a third-year teenager for help. The older boy led him to an unmarked door and directed George right into—SPLASH—a soapy mop bucket.

"This is just a janitor's closet!" George said.

"Welcome to Pilfer, kid!" the third-year called out as he fled.

So George wandered around the halls, squishing every time he took a step. After trudging across two rooms, George ran into an angry custodian who yelled at him for dripping brown water all over the nice floor—and wouldn't stop yelling until he shed his left shoe and sock. It was the second time he was forced to walk around Pilfer Academy of Filching Arts without a left shoe, since Ballyrag had stolen his other one, and he wondered how many days in a row he would go half shoeless.

He wandered around aimlessly, but the hallways were quite empty. It seemed as though everyone in the mansion had found their classes except him. George passed through an open, lofted hallway of grandfather clocks when the clocks struck 8:30 a.m., echoing so madly that George heard chimes for a solid minute after they had stopped ringing. He was officially late, and more lost than he had ever been.

But at the precise moment he was ready to give up, skip class, and wait in his room for someone to tell him what he missed, an adult wandered in.

"Oh, hello!" said a round man, nodding at George. The man was very short and very wide, with a face that was made up of just a bunch of chins and glasses that were far too big for him. He looked like a big-bellied bug.

"Excuse me!" George called, relieved to find someone who—he assumed—wouldn't direct him into a closet. "I'm looking for the Blackbeard Wing."

"The new student, I presume? George Beckett?"

George nodded.

"First-years . . . criminally hopeless," the man said, shaking his head. "Just round the corner there's a spiral staircase, go up two flights, walk straight about fifteen paces, and the Blackbeard Wing will be on your left-hand side."

"Thanks!" George said breathlessly, dashing toward the spiral staircase.

"Wait!" the man called.

George paused and turned around.

"You're missing a shoe."

"I know."

The man chuckled. "You're pretty strange, aren't you, kid?"

George ran around the corner, up the stairs, paced down the hall, and burst through the door of Blackbeard 204.

Ballyrag stood at the front of the class, but when he turned to George, his expression became panicked. "HELP!" Ballyrag shouted. "A THIEF IS BREAKING INTO MY CLASS! HIDE ALL THE VOLUBLES!"

"I'm not breaking in! I'm *supposed* to be here," George explained. "Remember? You kidnapped me?"

"Oh yes," Ballyrag said, then he fondly patted George's shoe, which he was still wearing around his neck. "Right.

Well then . . . you're late! One bajillion demerits for you! You can take a seat, Mr. Bucket."

"It's Beckett."

Ballyrag scratched his head.

George took a seat at the only empty desk, next to Tabitha, who leaned over and whispered faster than he had ever heard anyone speak, "There *are* no demerits, here. Just so you know. Only detentions and the whirly-blerg. You're lucky it's your first day because—believe me—you don't want either of those."

"Why not?" he hissed.

The corner of her mouth twitched as she looked up at the chalkboard, now covered with notes. "Quiet, or I'll lose my key!" she hissed.

"Lose your *what*?" George whispered, but Tabitha kicked him under the seat.

"—never do well if you don't think inside the box. But you all should feel very honored to be secluded among our ranks! As I was esplaining," Ballyrag said, "right now, we're going to be learning about basic grieving theory."

Tabitha raised her hand. "You mean *Thieving* Theory, right?" she called out.

Ballyrag grunted.

"So . . . let's start with kidnapping. What's the number

one thing you have to remember about that?" The class was silent, hanging on Ballyrag's answer. He sighed as though the answer was obvious. "You gotta remember to hold them for handsome."

Tabitha's hand shot up. "You mean *ransom*, right?" she shouted out.

Ballyrag grumbled.

She vigorously scribbled in her notebook.

"So when you're holding someone for handsome, you need to send them a list of reprimands—"

Once again, Tabitha's hand flew up, and she interrupted, "You mean *demands*, right?"

Ballyrag was starting to look annoyed—his nostrils flared out, and his eyes flashed angrily. He nodded brusquely before moving on with the lecture. "And you got to make sure your ransom note sounds very minister."

"You mean *sinister*, right?" she called out.

Ballyrag growled.

George leaned over to Tabitha. "Why do you keep correcting him?" he whispered.

"Why do you keep bothering me?"

"Why didn't you tell everyone I put the toast on Milo's chair?"

"I would never do anything that might even remotely help Milo," she said. "We are *not* friends."

"Why not?"

"Shhhhhhh!" she snapped.

"—a threat, a bequest, and constructions are the last things you need to remember to make a good letter." Ballyrag finished grandly, raising his hands in the air. He skulked to a cabinet on the other side of the classroom and retrieved supplies—scissors, construction paper, stacks of magazines, and rubber gloves. "We're going to make our own handsome notes, now, so get your magazines."

Milo rushed to the front of the room and accidentally-on-purpose knocked into George as he cut in front of him. At last, the line cleared out ahead, and George swiped a few magazines, a pair of scissors, a glue stick, construction paper, and rubber gloves. He returned to his desk and started on his project. He glanced over at Becca, who was the only one from his breakfast table that was sitting near him. She looked like she was having a grand old time poking holes through the magazine models' eyes.

George began to line up a few choice letters—mostly vowels—on his piece of orange construction paper. Then he found some threatening-looking consonants and began to form words. After ten minutes, he had pasted a short letter, and he was pretty satisfied with it.

He looked over at Tabitha, and she had already written what looked like a whole essay out of magazine snippets. He tried to see what she was gluing, but as soon as she caught on, she shot him a scandalized look, then hunched over her project and shielded her ransom note with her arm.

"I'm not copying!" George explained. "I'm done . . . and I'm bored."

Tabitha ignored him.

When Ballyrag finally called for an end to the project, Tabitha was still gluing. In fact, she glued and glued and glued while Ballyrag had the whole first row read their ransom notes aloud. Then it was the second row, and George was first.

"Mr. Bennett, your turn."

"Beckett," Tabitha corrected mindlessly, still gluing letters down.

George stood up with his paper, cleared his throat, and read:

I AM HOLDING YOUR KID HOSTAGE.
GIVE ME A MILLION DOLLARS OR ELSE.

"Sweet and short!" Ballyrag said, nodding. "But next time, you may want to give better defections." He threw a bit of dust on George's paper and wiped it with a brush.

It looked like the makeup brush his mom used to apply powder to her face.

George raised his hand. "What is that?"

"Fingerprinting powder and applercation brush. From my crime kit." Ballyrag finished blowing the dust off George's note, and not a fingerprint in sight. "All clear! Next!"

"Hold on, I'm not done gluing," Tabitha said. George thought that was bold of her, but everyone in the class let out a collective sigh.

Ballyrag cocked his head to the side in confusion, his mouth agape. George thought that if Ballyrag were a cartoon character, he would most certainly have a question mark hovering over his head at that moment.

"Okaaaaaayyyyy," Tabitha said, pressing down her last letter. "Ready!"

Tabitha read in a loud and dramatic voice:

I HAVE THE MOST IMPORTANT PERSON EVER
YES I HAVE STOLEN HIM MUAHAHAHAHA.
IF YOU EVER WANT HIM BACK
LEAVE A BILLION DOLLARS
ON THE CORNER WHERE CLINTON STREET
MEETS KINCAID AVENUE.

**IF YOU DON'T FOLLOW MY INSTRUCTIONS
YOU WILL NEVER SEE YOUR PRECIOUS
SON AGAIN.
MUAHAHAHAHAHAHA.**

"Very good, Miss Crawfish!"

"That's *Crawford*," Tabitha said.

Ballyrag coughed. "Good. Very pacific and clear. Nice villainous flair with the evil laughter."

After a while of listening to ransom notes, they all began to sound the same. And just as his last classmate had finished reading her note, the bell rang. George gathered up his books and followed Tabitha out of the classroom.

Their next class, Stealth 101, was on the other side of the mansion. No one waited for George—not even the kids he had breakfast with this morning—and so he walked alone.

At last, he arrived at the classroom, and George took the only available seat. Five minutes after class was supposed to begin, the teacher still hadn't arrived.

George glanced at his schedule again—someone named Browbeat was supposed to be teaching this class. If he or she ever showed up. George leaned over to his neighbor. "Is Browbeat usually late like this?"

The girl, who looked about as old as his sister Colby, rolled her eyes and ignored him.

"Boo!" said a voice, and George whipped around. There was a man standing against the wall—well, actually, more like blending into the wall. George hadn't even noticed him! The man wore a suit that matched the beige color of the classroom, and his face was painted to look like the art he stood in front of. As he walked to the front of the classroom, he took off his towering wig and wiped the makeup off with a handkerchief. George recognized him immediately. It was the round man with the many chins and enormous glasses that had given him directions to Ballyrag's class.

"I do this every time we have a new student," Browbeat said. "I was, indeed, here the whole time. I just want you to realize how unobservant you truly are."

George nodded.

"Though," Browbeat said, "I just talked to Dean Dean Deanbugle, who seems to think you are not lacking in areas of stealth and cunning. In fact, he says we should all expect great things from you. I think his exact word was: *exceptional.*"

George sunk down in his seat. He could feel people glaring at him, but he didn't dare look.

The class itself was rather dull. Browbeat lectured

for an hour and fifteen minutes on the basic principles of stealthiness, which he called the P-I-S-S method: Patience, Imperturbability, Silence, and Surprise. Of course, this resulted mostly in Milo and his two friends—Adam and Carrie, as George discovered from Browbeat's roll call—making *pssssssss* noises throughout the entire class underneath their breath.

At lunch, George ate with Robin, Neal, Beth, and Becca again. They kept talking about some funny thing that happened during one of their exams two months ago, and Neal was desperately trying to catch George up.

"So then the mice were loose and running all over the place, and the cats were going nuts in their cages—"

"Oh my goodness," Becca interrupted. "Remember that fat orange cat?"

Robin shuddered. "How could I—"

"Wait!" Neal said. "I'm explaining to George. So then, Strongarm released the cats from their cages, and they were running toward the mice. And some of the mice were getting eaten. It was pretty bloody, actually. Anyway, so I shouted, 'RUN, MICE! HIDE AND GO SQUEAK!'"

Robin burst into giggles and Beth snorted.

George smiled weakly.

"I . . . uh . . . guess you had to be there," Neal said, and then he turned back to Beth who was launching into the memory of what happened once during a detention they'd all shared.

George sighed and looked around the dining hall. Tabitha was sitting alone, and he thought about joining her, but when he caught her eye, she pointedly looked away.

George stood up, and a balding waiter took his plate.

"Thank you," George said.

The man looked entirely taken aback. He frowned like he was about to say something, but then he seemed to think better of it and scampered off to the kitchen, gripping George's dirty dish.

That afternoon, George arrived early to Practical Applications of Breaking and Entering. Strongarm was standing in the front of the blackboard.

Once everyone arrived, Strongarm broke the class up into two teams—everyone with an A–M name on one team, and everyone with an N–Z name on the other team. George was stuck with Milo, unfortunately, who began the session by puffing out his chest and boasting that he could handle *every* practical situation this class threw at him because he was top of the class.

"Not the top," a teenager named Jacob said. Jacob

looked significantly older than everyone else—he had the beginnings of a stubbly mustache on his upper lip. "Tabitha's top. Then Sunny, then Tiago, then Robin, *then* you."

Milo crossed his arms and scowled.

Strongarm retreated into a small door next to the blackboard—which seemed to lead into a storage closet—and rolled out two stage-prop doors in front of each team. One was a miniature door, made for a mouse, which George luckily got. The other team's door was the biggest door George had ever seen. It was at least twelve feet tall and ten feet wide and five feet thick.

"Whichever team can get through, over, or under this locked door first gets an A for the day!" Strongarm said.

Everyone groaned.

"An A?" Milo griped.

"An A and ice cream?" Strongarm suggested. "Studies have shown that children love ice cream."

"Keep talking," a small, blond boy shouted out.

"Oh . . . AHA!" Strongarm said, clearly coming to some sort of realization. "The winning team gets Triple-dipple Ultra-deluxe Melty Creamy Creamer Rainbow Swizzle Milk Munch ice cream. A whole tub of Triple-dipple

Ultra-deluxe Melty Creamy Creamer Rainbow Swizzle Milk Munch ice cream for each and every person on the winning team!"

The class hooted and hollered with excitement, George included. He still had *no* idea what a rainbow swizzle ice cream was, but after hearing Strongarm talk about it so often, he now had extremely high expectations.

The assignment was rather easy for George's team, who only had to step over the mouse-sized door to complete the task. But there was no way over, around, under, or through for the team that got the door built for a giant. The other team fiddled with the locks, but by the time they got a bobby pin ready, George's team had already won.

His entire team applauded, and even though he had been feeling down today, he couldn't help but cheer, too. Strongarm began to look around the classroom with shifty, darting eyes. "Uh . . . excuse me . . . gotta go get that . . . prize . . . ?" she squeaked before turning on her heels and bolting out of the classroom. She didn't return by the time the bell rang, which made George think that she was probably bluffing about that big stock of triple-dipple-whatever ice cream.

His last class of the day was Gadgetry with Pickapocket. Pickapocket was a wiry woman with bulging eyes and a creepy, unsettling smile. Her short, spiky hair was mussed in a hundred different directions, making her head look a bit like a pincushion. Her clothes were far too baggy, her pants far too short, and her glasses didn't even have lenses in them. George thought she looked a bit unhinged, and his suspicion was only confirmed when she started the class by throwing dental floss at them.

"ABSOLUTELY EVERYTHING," she squawked, "IS A GADGET."

They spent the whole class examining normal objects—dental floss, T-shirts, blankets, toothbrushes, candles, books, umbrellas, galoshes, stuffed animals, toilet paper—and talking about how these objects could help a thief. Eventually, Pickapocket promised as the class ended, they would get to some real high-level, intricate, state-of-the-art gizmo technology—but that wouldn't be until their second year.

"You've got to master the basics!" she cawed as everyone filed out of her class.

George had more homework than he had ever had in his entire life—an essay on the P-I-S-S method of stealth, a list on all the things he could do with a tissue box, and ten practice ransom notes all due the next day. Plus, he had a pop quiz in Practical Applications tomorrow, which Strongarm had told them was coming.

He spent a few hours at the library, finishing up his homework and trying not to get distracted by the second-years and third-years studying in groups. There was a lot more laughing than studying. George's heart felt a bit hollow watching them.

By the time he arrived back in the dorms after dinner, George's feet were sore and he was so exhausted he could collapse. He was panting when he reached the top of the penthouse, but when he opened the door to his room, he was breathless for a different reason.

His mattress, blankets, and pillows were nowhere to be seen. Where a full bed should have been, there was only the wooden bed frame. He walked over and found a note on the headboard:

Don't even think about that key, new kid.

Sleep tight.

George instantly whipped around to Milo—but Milo was either fast asleep or pretending to be. He couldn't even *believe* how nasty Milo was being to him. They were roommates, which meant they were supposed to get along, or—at the very least—be able to live in the same room in peace. George had shared a room all his life, and Milo was making his wrestle-mania, headlock-loving brother, Gunther, look like a saint.

George trudged to the rooftop garden terrace and leaned against the balcony, watching the stars blink. It was a beautiful night—the air was warm and the valley stretched out below in the shadow of the moon—but he was completely miserable.

What in the world was he going to *do*? He couldn't stay here. He clearly didn't belong. But escape didn't even seem possible with that enormous wall surrounding all the gardens and courtyard. Like a prison wall.

You just have to get used to living here, George told himself. *You don't have a choice.* But that didn't make him feel any better.

There was a shuffling sound, and George whipped around. Tabitha was behind him.

"What's wrong?" Tabitha asked curiously.

George folded his arms. He didn't want her to know how upset he felt, but he couldn't keep it in. He took a deep breath and said, "My mattress and pillow were stolen."

"Of course they were," Tabitha said, rolling her eyes. "It's a *thieving* school. What did you expect?"

George frowned. Couldn't she at least pretend to feel

bad for him? He irritably crumpled the note he'd found on his headboard.

"What's that you've got there?" Tabitha said, looking down at his hands.

He handed her the crinkly paper. "What's a key?" he asked.

Tabitha peered at the paper and shook her head. When she finally spoke, her voice was surprisingly soft. "The top five students in each class get a key to the Robin Hood Room. The teachers are always tweaking the rankings, so people lose and gain access to the lounge every few weeks."

"And what's a hurly curl? Burly girl? Wergy lurl?"

"The whirlyblerg. It's Dean Dean Deanbugle's signature punishment."

"What is it?"

"You think *I'd* know? I've never gotten in trouble!" Tabitha looked out over the terrace thoughtfully. "But to be honest, I don't think anyone really knows what it is. People who go there usually don't come back."

George leaned against the balcony and sighed. All he wanted was to go home—to where he never had to think about horrible roommates or keys or Robin Hood Rooms or whirly-whatevers ever again.

"Tabitha, how long does it take to get used to this place?"

"You'll like it here eventually—everyone does. I promise."

BRRRRRRRRING! came the sound of a bell.

"Oh, that's the curfew alarm! Don't stay out here too late, or you might get in trouble." She walked over to the exit. "Good night, George," she said, and she shut the door behind her.

Nothing Is Beneath a Thief

The next evening, George stole Milo's bedding—his mattress, sheets, comforter, and pillow. The plan was to be
fast asleep by the time Milo returned, so that it would
be impossible to covertly steal the bedding back while
George was wrapped up in it. George had to go to bed at
7:00 p.m. to pull this off, but it was worth it. The next
morning his own bedding had mysteriously returned,
and Milo looked steamed. George counted that as his
first victory.

The two weeks after that passed surprisingly quickly.
Classes kept him very busy. After they mastered ransom-
note writing in Thieving Theory, George and his classmates moved on to different types of get-rich-quick
schemes. Ballyrag taught them all about online phish-
ing (which Ballyrag kept confusing with real-live, boat-

in-the-water fishing), in which you'd e-mail someone pretending that their credit card accounts were about to be deactivated and ask for all of their personal, private information.

It was all a bit complicated, but George thought he had a good handle on the material. A few people were very lost and kept mixing up the players of the scheme until Ballyrag was so confused by all of their confusion that he scratched his head silently for the last fifteen minutes of class.

Pickapocket had finally advanced them from dental floss to toothpaste, and Browbeat's Stealth class required them to stand in one place for an hour without making a sound, which George *almost* passed—except for a tiny little sneeze after fifty-three minutes. The average fail time was around thirty-five minutes, and only Tabitha passed the sixty-minute mark. She had gone sixty-four minutes before she sighed a little too loudly, but hers was still the record to beat. George wasn't sure he liked Stealth class. Standing rigidly for an hour wasn't exactly *fun*.

He did like Strongarm's class, though, which was full of lock picking, safe opening, obstacle courses, and races. But the class would have been a lot better if he didn't feel like he was being hazed by Milo and his friends. It seemed like they were always going out of their way to mess him up. During one drill—a tag relay race where each team had to transport a bag of fake diamonds through an obstacle course—Milo, who was on George's team, threw the bag so far to the left that George fell into a mud pit diving for the catch.

At first he thought it was an accident, but when Milo started snickering and high-fiving his other teammates, George realized with a sinking feeling that they were trying to sabotage him. He picked himself up, mud-soaked and dripping, and continued his mission to pass the diamond bag to Sunny, the next teammate in the relay line.

At the end of class, Strongarm announced their scores aloud. "George, full marks for your fortitude, willingness to dive into mud, determination to save the mission, and for not fumbling the catch. Dean Dean Deanbugle was most certainly right about you!"

"Are you *kidding me*?" Carrie complained loudly at the end of class. "Even when he goes off course, he *still* gets a perfect score."

George flushed. He didn't know how to respond, but Tabitha interjected. "Why don't you gossip a little louder?" she snarled. "There's probably someone in the village down the hill who couldn't hear you." Carrie looked at Tabitha like she'd slapped her.

George caught up to Tabitha in the hallway. "Thanks," he said, but she folded her arms.

"Jealousy, George."

"Huh?"

"They're just jealous because you're the dean's new favorite," she said with a curt nod. "Just ignore them."

She hurried off, disappearing behind a crowd of second-years. George stood glued to the spot for a few minutes afterward, half confused and half stunned. Why wouldn't Tabitha talk to him for more than a second?

On Friday night, after spending the evening finishing up a Stealth class essay in the Butch Cassidy Wing, George headed to the dining hall for a bite of dinner. But as he turned the corner, he stumbled right into Dean Dean Deanbugle himself.

"George, m'boy!" the dean said, holding his bowl of bow tie pasta steady. "Just the pupil I'm looking for! May I have a word?"

George checked his silver watch—only fifteen minutes until the dining hall closed for the night. His stomach gave a violent gurgle, but he said, "Um, sure."

He followed Dean Dean Deanbugle to his office again, where the full-length windows showed a very hazy-looking dusk. The dean took a seat behind his desk, and George sat in a chair in front of him.

"I just wanted to check in with you—to see how you are acclimating to your environment here. Your teachers have been giving you top marks."

George shrugged.

"Well?" the dean said, his wild eyebrows dancing. "How do you like Pilfer Academy?"

George hesitated. "It's all right, I guess."

Dean Dean Deanbugle laughed so loud that he practically shook the room. "I don't suppose you've heard anything about the midterm?"

George had. Even though it was only the beginning of August, it seemed like he couldn't escape the whispers and rumors about the upcoming September midterm. Each "year" went on a different excursion, and every midterm was different from the one before. Neal had told him all about last semester's attempt to steal a bunch of pets to create a private Pilfer zoo. And for the midterm last March, Becca said the first-years went on a jewel heist. And before that, they went to a theme park and stole all the mascot costumes.

"I've heard rumors," George finally said.

"I don't expect you'll have any problems, but I do think—should you want a hint—I could give it to you."

"But Dean Dean Deanbugle—isn't that cheating?" George said.

"Cheating, schmeating," the dean said, waggling his eyebrows. "What's the number one rule of thieving?"

"Finders keepers, losers weepers?" George guessed.

"No. Well, yes. Well, that *is* a top rule of thieving. But the number one rule is that nothing is off limits. Nothing is beneath a thief."

"Nothing?"

"Nothing," said the dean, stroking his chin. "Except maybe the ground. That's pretty much always beneath a thief."

George paused. Extra help *would* be nice, and the dean *was* offering . . . but then again, he was already getting too much attention from Dean Dean Deanbugle. If he took extra help from the dean, he'd create a lot more enemies. And the last thing he needed was more enemies.

"No thanks," George said. "I want to prove that I can make it on my own. I don't need any extra help."

"I daresay you don't!" said the dean. "Well, you'll know where to find me if you change your mind. I'll just be in my office . . . or on the grounds . . . or in my bedroom tower . . . or in the dining hall . . . or in a classroom . . . or wandering the halls . . . or in the library . . . or in the gardens . . . or in another teacher's office . . . or hiding in a nook or cranny . . . or out on an important thieving mission . . . or tending the whirlyblerg . . . or eating gnocchi . . ."

"Thank you," George interrupted, because he was still *soooooo hungry*, and it didn't seem like the dean was going to stop talking any time soon. "That's good to know."

The dean licked his finger and brushed his hairy eyebrows with his thumb. He stared at George pensively for a moment, and his smile fell from his face. "Get out of my office."

"What?"

"Get out," the dean said firmly.

George stammered. "B-but what—why—"

"We are done here. NOW LEAVEEEEEEE," the dean howled.

George scrambled out of the dean's office. As he swiveled out from around the moving bookcase, he tumbled smack into Milo. They both went sprawling on the ground, and a drinking glass went rolling across the floor and into the hall.

"Milo! What are you doing here?"

Milo glared. He wore a sour expression, like someone was wafting a poo popsicle beneath his nose. "You like being the new favorite, Beckett?"

"What are you talking about?" George asked. But Milo just glared at him.

George rolled his eyes and began to walk away.

"You won't be his pet for long!" Milo blurted. "The teachers always move on to the newest, freshest student. So don't feel special or anything. He'll never offer you help on a midterm again!"

How would Milo know what the dean just said? George thought. *Unless . . .*

He gasped. "You were holding that glass against the door, weren't you? Trying to listen in on my meeting with Dean Dean Deanbugle!"

"So what if I was?" Milo said, puffing up like an angry cat. "You think you're so much better than me? Well, you're not. I'm better than you . . . and everyone else in this place. You'll see!"

"I don't think I'm better than you! I never said that!" George protested. Then his stomach growled, and he skirted around Milo. "I'm way too hungry to deal with you right now."

He bolted, leaving Milo clenching his fists. George ran as fast as he could back to the dining hall, only to find the doors locked.

"Noooooooooooooooo!" George cried.

He banged, bashed, beat, battered, pounded, thudded, *hammered* on the doors until his fists were red raw and aching.

He finally slumped against the doors in defeat. "Let me in! Please!"

"I-I'm very sorry, but dining hours are over," said a small voice from the other side of the closed door.

A waitress! George perked up. "Please *pleaseeeeee* make one exception! I swear I won't tell anyone you let me in—I haven't eaten since noon! And we were running laps in Strongarm's class today!"

"I—I'm really, really sorry. I can't. We'll all get in a lot of trouble."

"Trouble?"

"Whirly—" she cut off, then cleared her throat stiffly. "Tomorrow's Saturday, so the dining hall opens at ten. Come back then."

From the other side of the door, he could hear her scuttle away.

Could someone really get sent to the whirlyblerg if they bent the rules a little to feed a student? George didn't know what to think about that. Mostly, he felt bad for the waitstaff.

An enormous groan came from his gut. Fourteen more hours until the dining hall opened again, and his stomach was already having a hissy fit.

This was going to be the *worst night ever.*

As Long as You Don't Get Caught

That night, George tried to go to sleep, but he woke up a few hours later, so hungry he was actually in pain. He rustled through his drawers for any remainders of food. *I have to start a snack stash*, he thought as his stomach became a gurgling, burbling symphony.

At last, George quietly left his room, careful not to wake Milo, whose snores were reminiscent of a lovesick goose.

Four flights down, he was back in the open area with the row of couches—and, of course, the big door that led into the hall. He walked out and gently closed the door behind him.

Then he turned to face the long, shadowy hall. There was no turning back now. Unless, of course, he decided to turn back.

George crept cautiously in the darkness. All throughout the hall, he did his best to be sneaky. He hugged the wall like a ninja. He slinked like a Slinky. He slid like a shortstop. He crouched and slunk and tiptoed and crawled and lurked and inched and slithered.

Suddenly, someone tapped his shoulder.

"AHHHHHHHHH!" he screamed, whipping around.

It was Tabitha, wearing a black woolen cap and a ski mask. "Shhhhhhhhh!" She put a hand over his mouth. "You know, you're not as sneaky as you think you are."

"Mmmm mmm mmm mmmmm?" George tried to talk through her hands. She let go of his face, and he repeated himself. "What are you doing?"

"Following you!" she whispered. "Clearly."

"Well, turn back."

She shook her head. "It's too late now. I'm already out. Can I—can I come?"

George sighed. He didn't really see what choice he had. Now that Tabitha caught him, he didn't want her running to a teacher to tattle on him. "Okay. I guess so," he relented.

They continued along the corridor in silence, shuffling across the Persian rug that lay atop the shiny wood floor.

"So where are we going?" Tabitha whispered.

"The kitchen," George said, just as his stomach gave a droning, moaning groan. "I skipped dinner."

"I know," Tabitha said, creeping over to the stairs. "You were talking to the dean after he invited you to his office."

"How'd you—"

"Please," she said. "Everyone's talking about it. Robin and Neal were *convinced* you were getting bumped to the next grade. But obviously that's impossible, since no one gets moved up that fast. And Milo started this ridiculous rumor that you were getting expelled. But that's just what he wants to happen. He's crazy competitive."

"I know! He followed me to Dean Dean Deanbugle's office and eavesdropped on us. Then he tried to fight with me about it! How does he even have the time to be so obsessed with beating me? Doesn't he have homework or something?"

Tabitha sighed. "When I first arrived at Pilfer, Milo, Carrie, and Adam were actually really nice to me . . ."

"Milo? Nice?" George said incredulously. He was so surprised that he almost ran into a marble column. He artfully dodged it at the last moment.

Tabitha chuckled. "Well, *now* I know better. For a few weeks, I was friends with him and his group. But in July they gave out rankings, and I was number one. Milo pretended to be really supportive, but a few days later—the night before we had a big Thieving Theory project due and a Gadgetry test—someone snuck into my room, stole all of my class binders, and ripped all of my work to shreds. I had to start the project all over again from scratch, and I stayed up all night to do it. I couldn't finish it in time, though, and I failed the Gadgetry test because I fell asleep on question three. Milo had a big laugh about it at dinner in front of everyone."

George's jaw dropped.

"Oh, but it wasn't just him. Other people were trying to sabotage me, too. It's really hard to trust anyone when you're ranked number one," she said sadly. "I can never tell if people are being nice to me because they're actually good people—or because they want me to let my guard down again, so they can stab me in the back."

George suddenly felt like he wanted to hug Tabitha. Her time at Pilfer Academy sounded really lonely.

"Why are you telling me all this?" George asked.

"I honestly don't know," she said. "I suppose . . . I feel like I can trust *you*. I remember better than anyone what it's like to be the new kid, since I'm still pretty new myself. And I guess I just can't imagine you trying to sabotage anyone. I've noticed how you are—in class and in the dining hall and in the dorm. You're pretty nice . . . for a criminal-in-training." She started to laugh, but then she put her hands over her mouth, looking around to make sure the coast was still clear.

As they prowled into the Sundance Kid Wing in silence, George smiled. It felt good, talking with Tabitha. Maybe it was because they were both new and didn't have to catch each other up on inside jokes. Or maybe it was because she always seemed to have his back. Even when she was trying to be a loner, she was still acting like a friend.

"Do you like it here yet?" she asked suddenly.

He looked at her and grinned. "I think I'm starting to. You?"

"I *love* it here! I'm getting the education of a lifetime!"

George laughed.

"Seriously! Pilfer is the best school of its kind, and I'm being challenged in every way possible. Physically, mentally, emotionally—it's all such an amazing way to grow!"

"I guess I never really thought of it like that."

Tabitha turned to him. There was a hunger in her eyes akin to the hunger he was feeling in the pit of his stomach, which gurgled again. "I'm going to be the *best*. In anything, everything, and especially this."

"Sounds like a lot of pressure," George said.

"Really? I think it's fun."

They reached a corner, and Tabitha peeked first while George guarded the flank. When they determined the coast was clear, they continued forward, walking through a room with rather creaky wood floors.

"Shhh!" George said.

"Shhhhhh!" Tabitha hissed back.

"Shhhhhhhhhhhhhh!"

"Shhhhhhhhhhhhhhhhhhhhh!"

"No, really!" George said. "I think I hear something."

Quickly, George pulled Tabitha behind a long window curtain, and they stood rigidly against the wall. There came a *CREEEEEEFAAAAAAKKKK* and a *WAAAAAAAAAH-HHHH* and then nothing. George's heart thudded like pounding footsteps.

"It's just the mansion settling in," Tabitha said after a moment, but George thought she sounded a bit unsure. "Just the sounds of an old house."

They peeked out—the coast was clear.

They walked a bit more carefully now, pausing to look behind them every so often. Finally, they made their way into the Autolycus Wing, ever closer to the kitchen.

When they reached the kitchen door, Tabitha stepped up. She took out two wires from her pocket and began fiddling with the lock. Within moments, it clicked, and the door swung open.

"If they didn't want us breaking in, they shouldn't start teaching us how to pick locks in the first year," Tabitha said, rolling her eyes.

Inside, the kitchen was positively *glorious*. There were rows and rows of foods of all kinds: crackers and cheeses and pastas and cereals and granola bars and fruits and breads and syrups and sauces and pretzels and chips and cookies, cookies, cookies—a full two rows of floor-to-ceiling cookies.

But George and Tabitha went right to the freezer. In the very corner, buried under pounds of uncooked lamb chops, they found *exactly* what they were looking for: a carton of Triple-dipple Ultra-deluxe Melty Creamy Creamer Rainbow Swizzle Milk Munch ice cream.

"YES!" Tabitha squealed, running to grab two spoons. "I've been waiting to try this for the last three months. You have *no idea* how often Strongarm taunts us with this."

"Cheers," said George, clinking his spoon on Tabitha's, and then they both dug into the carton.

The ice cream was a taste-splosion of flavors in his mouth. At first, it was cool and light, perfect for a hot summer's day, but then it became heavy and sweet, like a decadent dessert after an enormous feast. Then, it was like he was tasting colors: A punch of red, a kick of green, a buzz of yellow, a smack of purple, a burst of orange, a whack of turquoise, a wallop of magenta. Then came the munch of the cookie pieces inside. It was creamy and crunchy and melty and dribbly drippy soft.

George had never, ever, *ever* in his entire life tasted something so delicious.

"Oh my *goodness*," Tabitha said, her eyes wide. She reached in for another spoonful, and George did, too. But just before he could take that second bite, the door to the kitchen opened.

"QUICK! HIDE!" Tabitha whispered. They scurried behind a wall of cereal boxes. There was just enough of a crack between them to see a long bathrobe shuffle close, close, close, too close, dangerously close, deathly close to where they were.

"Hello? Helloooooo!" called Strongarm's voice, just feet away from where they hid. "I know you're in here," Strongarm said loudly. The footsteps paced the kitchen, and her voice echoed around the shelves. "Is someone here? Maybe? Possibly? Or perhaps not . . ." She walked to the door, her footsteps growing fainter.

GURGLE GRUMBLE BURGLY BURBLE GURGLEY GOO, shouted George's stomach.

Tabitha elbowed him, but it was too late. The damage was done.

Strongarm whipped around and clomped toward them with renewed vigor. The look on her face was wild, like a panther on the prowl.

"Stay," hissed Tabitha in George's ear. "I can get us out of this. I'm a smooth talker."

"No—"

But she crawled out from behind the shelf anyway. "Strongarm!" Tabitha gasped. "What are *you* doing here?"

"No, what are *you* doing here?" said Strongarm.

"I asked first."

"But I'm older."

"Age before beauty," Tabitha said sweetly. Then she smiled widely and gave Strongarm a little wink.

Strongarm floundered. "Why, I was responding to the silent alarm that went off when the kitchen door opened."

Silent alarm! George thought.

"Oh," Tabitha said, putting on a sulking voice. "I was planning an enormous food heist so that I could impress you. But I guess my plan is foiled."

"Humph!" Strongarm humphed. "It is foiled, indeed. Well, head on back to bed. I'll have to have a word with

Browbeat about teaching you to be more successfully stealthy. What in the world—" She spotted the carton of ice cream and spluttered.

George began to sweat.

"TWO SPOONS! OF MY OWN PERSONAL STASH OF TRIPLE-DIPPLE ULTRA-DELUXE MELTY CREAMY CREAMER RAINBOW SWIZZLE MILK MUNCH ICE CREAM! TWO SPOONS! TWO! SPOONS!"

"One for each hand," Tabitha boasted.

"TWO DETENTIONS! ONE FOR EACH SPOON!"

There were some scuffling noises and yelps and arguing, and then their footsteps grew fainter and fainter until they were gone.

George crawled out of his hiding spot and finished the open carton of melting ice cream. He couldn't help but smile. A thrilling adventure, a new friend, *and* delicious ice cream? He could definitely get used to this.

Class Rankings

For days, George felt excited whenever he thought about the kitchen raid. It had been exhilarating—the adrenaline rush, the fear of getting caught, the tension, the danger! He'd never pulled off anything like it before. For the first time since he'd arrived, George felt like thief school might be perfect for him after all.

He was so proud of himself that even poor Tabitha's detention couldn't dampen his good mood.

Tabitha tried to keep the details of her detention a secret, but after a few days of relentless questioning, George finally wore her down at lunch.

"Okay, fine! You win!" she said. She looked around to make sure that the table of third-years behind them wasn't listening in. "In the basement, they have a room . . ." She trailed off as she slurped up a spoonful of matzo ball soup.

"And?"

"Well, it's a pool filled with piranhas," she said with her mouth full.

George's jaw dropped. "They put you in a pool of piranhas? That's—that's *inhumane!*"

"Of course they didn't drop me in a pool of piranhas—that would be ridiculous. I had to brush their teeth."

"You *brushed* their *teeth?*"

"Apparently Strongarm takes oral hygiene very seriously."

George laughed, and Tabitha tried not to smile.

"It's so not funny—their teeth are *sharp*," she said. "But do you want to hear something weird? Strongarm was supervising me, but then Ballyrag came in and said there was someone on the asparagus for her."

"On the what?"

Tabitha poked a matzo ball with her spoon. "Asparagus. At least, that's what I thought I heard. Then Strongarm and Ballyrag both left for a while. That's when I did the bulk of the brushing. It was really rather terrifying. Still," she said dreamily, "it was so worth it for a bite of that ice cream. When can we raid the kitchen again?"

"Soon," George promised. "But let's not get caught next time."

"Deal!"

He took a sip of his milkshake. It was, sadly, not even half as good as Triple-dipple Ultra-deluxe Melty Creamy Creamer Rainbow Swizzle Milk Munch ice cream. But he wondered if *anything* would hold its own against that perfection. He couldn't wait to try another bite.

But he didn't get the chance in the week that followed. George soon found himself buried under mountain loads of homework.

Every day after class, Tabitha dashed off to study in the library for a few hours before dinner. But George found the library to be a bit stuffy, so on those rare occasions when they had to work silently, he had taken to study-ing in his room, or in the tiny nooks he found around the school, like a window seat in the Blackbeard Wing that overlooked a valley of trees, or an enormous couch he found in an attic room. He even made it back to the plushy chair in the greenhouse. He loved looking at all the exotic plants from around the world, though he was careful to avoid the poisonous ones.

But sometimes he couldn't avoid the intimidating library. In the last week of August, George headed there during lunch to look at a few books for his project for Ballyrag—a binder on how to break into the Natural History Museum, complete with sections for the Intro-duction, Method, Purpose, Hypothesis, and Diagrams, which would have to include a full map of the Natural History Museum and another map of the getaway across New York City. The project wasn't due for a week, but since George had never been to New York City before, it was going to take a lot of research.

He climbed the ladder to the second story and began to look around the shelves, but he couldn't seem to find anything he was looking for. He passed Shakespeare and the Magna Carta, then he wiggled his way through the section on Pablo Picasso, and bypassed a section on the Federalist Papers. He stopped when he saw something that resembled the original subway plan for New York City from 1902. He went to take a book off the shelf, forgetting for a moment that it was chained to the wall.

George sighed a frustrated sigh. He tried to copy down notes, but it was a lot to juggle—a book, notebook, and a pen. After a dropping all three multiple times, he let out a groan. He'd probably do better climbing downstairs and working the assignment for Pickapocket's class: an essay on fifteen different uses for a toilet plunger.

"You'll have to steal a podium if you want to work in the library," a second-year girl passing by suggested to him. "There's no way you can juggle all that."

"Where do I find a podium to steal?"

She smirked. "Keep your eyes peeled, kid. Treasures are everywhere," she said, walking away.

Before George knew it, it was time for Practical Applications of Breaking and Entering. As he approached the classroom, he saw all of his classmates crowded around a piece of paper tacked up to a corkboard, everyone pushing and pulling and elbowing one another in an attempt to get closer to the front.

"What's going on?" George asked.

Neal turned to him. "It's our new class rankings—hey! Stop shoving me, Sunny!" And he rammed into her in response.

As Carrie attacked Becca, and Beth kicked Adam, and Tosh tripped Jacob, George moved closer to the list.

Big letters at the top of the paper said "NEW First Year Class Rankings," and below was a list of numbers and names:

156	Tabitha Crawford
5,483	George Beckett
78	Sunny Knight
4	Robin Gold
725	Tiago Martinez
17,000,000 and ½	Milo Hubervick

5	Ezra Steinberg
111,222,333	Neal Fowler
32,840	Jacob Yates
999	Yuna Saito
0	Rebecca Ratcliffe
Infinity	Beth Ratcliffe
8	Sarah Kaide-Bradley
13,131	Carrie Parker
-20	Adam Hannon
15	Tosh Gupta

He wasn't sure how to understand this list. Five thousand four hundred and eighty-three. Was that . . . good? Or bad? What did it even mean?

Out of nowhere, something smacked him on the head.

"What the—!"

He ducked as Milo's fist came barreling his way again.

"What are you doing?!" George cried, backing up into Becca and Carrie's brawl. His butt sent them barreling into Jacob, who was now sitting on Tosh's head.

George turned toward Milo, who was all red-faced and sweaty.

"That's *my* spot you took."

George looked all around him and backed up a step.

"There's plenty of space to stand! No need to *hit* me!"

"That's not what I—"

"STOP FIGHTING!" Strongarm bellowed, and they all froze exactly where they stood—mid-headlock, mid-punch, and mid-kick. Strongarm sniffed. "Every single time a new ranking comes out . . . You ought to be ashamed, fighting like this." She shook her head disappointedly. "Why, you should *never* fight in public when you could anonymously attack later! Don't you know a thing or two about sneak revenge by now?"

Everyone grumbled insincere apologies.

"All right," Strongarm said, clapping her hands. "Let's file into the classroom! Come on!"

As everyone began to march inside, George approached his teacher. "Strongarm, what do the rankings mean?"

"Silly child," she said. "I should think this is self-explanatory. I mean, I made the list myself, and *I* had no trouble with it." Strongarm rubbed her pointy chin thoughtfully. "In fact," she continued, "if I were to make a test on reading this list, I would most certainly score a hundred percent."

"Well, of course you would," George said, "you made the list! And the test! But how do you expect anyone else to read it? Your numbers are in the wrong order."

"They are in precisely the order I put them in," Strongarm said, waggling a long, spindly finger. "Which means they are in the correct order."

"I don't think that's how numbers work."

"Numbers?" Strongarm chuckled. "What are you talking about, George? Thieves don't need numbers!"

"But you need to be able to count the money you've stolen, right?" George said.

"Pishposh! That's what you kidnap an accountant for!"

"But seriously, how—"

"Don't worry . . . the numbers are worthless," Tabitha said, peeking her head out of the classroom. "The only thing that matters is how close you are to the top of the page. The closer you are to the top of the page, the higher ranked you are . . . and the bottom of the list is, well, bottom ranked."

George strained, trying to remember where exactly his name was on the list. He whipped around to look again.

Two.

He was number two.

George scampered into the classroom and looked around at his classmates. Robin was proud, Neal seemed disappointed, and Becca and Beth acted like they were too cool to care. A few people looked satisfied, some angry, some determined, and those at the bottom of the list looked awfully nervous.

Tabitha seemed confident, and as he looked at her, she pulled on a piece of string around her neck, revealing a key. She dangled it in front of him and grinned.

At that moment, Dean Dean Deanbugle popped into their classroom.

"Hello!" he said, little bits of his ravioli lunch flying from his mouth. "Strongarm, I wondered if I might take over your class for a little while."

"Go right ahead," she said with a curtsy.

"Right, but you don't have to stay here." The dean looked around shiftily. "You can go to the *you-know-where* and use the *you-know-what*."

"What do I know?"

"The *asparagus*," Dean Dean Deanbugle whispered loudly. He looked at her pointedly.

Strongarm's eyes lit up. "MY LUCKY DAY!" she cried, and she skipped out of the classroom.

George looked at Tabitha and shrugged, which was his way of saying, *What was that about?*

She rolled her eyes, which was her way of saying, *Adults are WEIRD.*

With Strongarm gone, the dean paced around the front of the room, stealing glances with students one by one.

And from those glances, George could instantly tell how the dean felt about his classmates. At moments, Dean Dean Deanbugle looked positively furious: his mouth pulled in a hard, tight line; his nostrils shook violently; his thick eyebrows converged on his face, making his forehead look like a giant carpet. He glared at Adam and Carrie with pure disgust, with utter loathing, with the worst scowl that anyone could ever give another human being, and George thought it was a wonder that they didn't burst into tears. Then the dean grinned as he looked at Tabitha. He gave a grim nod to Neal and Ezra. He shook his head disappointedly at Milo. He clearly refused to even look at Tosh. And when the dean *finally* caught George's eye, he actually winked.

"Keys, please," Dean Dean Deanbugle said, at last, holding out his hand. Tabitha, Robin, Tiago, and Sunny walked to the front of the classroom and gave Dean Dean Deanbugle back their keys.

Milo did not get up from his seat.

"Mr. Hubervick," Dean Dean Deanbugle said sternly.

Milo clutched his key, his face turning redder than a baked ham. "I . . . this is *my* key."

"Not anymore," the dean said coolly, marching over to Milo's desk and wrenching the key from his hands.

"I've never lost a key before!" Milo said loudly. "It's

mine, and I deserve it more than anyone else—especially the new kids. I was number one for five months in a row. I should be moved up to second year!"

"You *were* number one for your first five months. But you're not anymore. You've been slipping down the ranks, and if you can't keep up with your classmates, you'll fall further still," Dean Dean Deanbugle said. "Now *quiet!* Or it's off to the whirlyblerg with you!"

Milo didn't say another word, but he shot a nasty glare at George.

Then, one-by-one, Dean Dean Deanbugle began to call the top five students up to receive their keys. After Tiago, Robin, and Sunny, it was George's turn.

He walked up to the front of the room, feeling like he almost had to shield his eyes from Dean Dean Deanbugle's dazzling smile. At last, he reached the dean, shook hands, and took his key.

"I'm very proud of you, George," Dean Dean Deanbugle said, clapping him on the shoulder and beaming. George could feel his ears turning pink, but he was more tickled than embarrassed. In fact, as he walked back to his seat, his grin was wider than a crater. He didn't even care that Milo was staring at him with a murderous gleam in his eye. He felt lighter than a balloon soaring up, up, up into the clouds.

George spent the whole class period—and all after-noon, really—holding the key in the palm of his hand and smiling.

After Gadgetry class, Tabitha grabbed him by wrist and dragged him down three flights of stairs. On the ground floor, she pulled him into the barren Ma Barker Wing, and George quickly realized that they were headed in the direction of the dead end on the first floor.

Tabitha stopped in the middle of the hall.

"Here we are!" Tabitha said with a squeal. "Welcome to the Robin Hood Room!"

"Where?" George said. Clearly Tabitha had gone insane—the corridor was completely empty, except for the weird cleaning supply and vegetable storage closet.

"Look at the wall, George. Pay attention."

He examined the wall. It looked ordinary—but then he realized that there was an area that was just a shade lighter than the rest of the hall. And the lighter part was in the tall, rectangular shape of a door.

"It's a door," George said, tracing the edge with his fingertips. There was a tiny keyhole, smack dab in the middle. "This is amazing! It blends right in!"

"If you think that's the amazing part," Tabitha said, "then I can't *wait* to see your face once we go in!"

She slid her key into the hole and turned it to the

left; the wall opened up to reveal a turnstile. She strode through and disappeared into the darkness beyond. The door automatically locked behind her. Then it was George's turn. He put his key into the slot, turned, and stepped through the turnstile.

The barrier moved, pushing him forward into a pitch-black hallway.

WHUMP. The door closed behind him.

He couldn't see or hear anything. "Tabitha?"

Silence pounded in his ears, and he could feel his heart thumping in his throat. He blinked hard, but there was nothing to see except darkness.

"Tabitha?! Where are you?"

"George," she said, and she was *right* next to him. "Walk forward."

He tentatively took a step forward, and the hallway suddenly lit up with a ring of fire that extended down the hall as far as he could see. The floor twinkled with a golden glow, illuminating a path to follow.

"Wow!" he whispered.

He leaped forward, and Tabitha ran behind him, laughing like he'd never heard her laugh before.

At the end of the hallway of encircling fire, there was a door. And through the door was a room with a trampoline floor.

"AWESOME!" George shouted as he jumped into the room and sprung back up. He and Tabitha bounced all the way across the room; on the other side, they bounced off the trampoline into a foam pit. They wiggled through the foam pit, which led to a slide, and the slide slithered down into a swimming pool and hot tub.

Each room was better than the last. There was an Unlimited Junk Food Room, with vending machines that were twelve feet tall and cabinets stocked with all sorts of sugary treats. There was a graffiti room, where kids were allowed to write whatever they wanted (even inappropriate words!) all over the walls in markers and spray paint. Then they popped into a space with a swing set and a floor piled with cushions—so students could jump off the swings and land in a pile of soft, fluffy goodness. There was even a room just for laser tag.

George's eyes grew wider and wider at the sight of it all. The Robin Hood Room was more wonderful than he'd ever imagined. It was better than recess, better than roller coasters, better than anything he'd ever experienced in his whole life. Because there were no rules—only play.

Pilfer Academy had always felt grand and cold, like a stodgy museum. But the Robin Hood Room—*this* was a room built just for fun!

"No wonder everyone wants to be in the top five," George said. "This is *amazing*!"

"Welcome to paradise," Tabitha said with a grin, and they ran giggling back to the candy room to stuff their faces with sweets.

Dastardly Plans! *Muahahaha!*

"I just want to be jumping on that trampoline," George said with a sigh in Strongarm's class the next day. He jiggled the combination lock on a small safe, which he was expected to break into by the end of the class period.

"Concentrate on cracking your safe," Tabitha said. "You have to stay on top, or you'll lose your key, and then you'll *never* be able to jump on that trampoline."

George smirked. "You're too intense."

"You're not intense enough," she muttered, then she let out a frustrated growl. "This stupid safe *won't crack*."

"You're too impatient," George said. On the other side of the room, Strongarm was breathing down Neal's neck as he spun his lock around. "You have to listen for the click, Tabitha . . . then it's two numbers to the right."

"I know that. I just don't hear a click!"

"Are you pushing up on the clamp?"

"Yes," she said through gritted teeth. "Okay, let's try this again." She pushed up on her lock and began to twist gingerly, her ear right up against the safe.

Strongarm stood up again and began to hawk the room, swooping down upon students unexpectedly. She kept standing uncomfortably close to people, shrieking "TICK! TICK! TICK! TICK! TICK! BOOM!" just to see how people would perform under pressure.

So far, the answer was not very well. Everyone she had attacked had started sweating log flumes, and Adam even burst into tears.

Tabitha groaned. "It's so hard to hear with Strongarm screaming like that. How are you doing?"

"I keep losing it by the third number," George said. "Now I have to start all over." He shook his box violently, and something very loud rattled around inside. From two tables over, Milo scowled at them, then turned back to his own safe with a sulky expression.

"It's not *our* fault he's number six," Tabitha said, rolling her eyes. "Ah—wait! I got the second one!" She scribbled down the second number to the combination lock. "One more to go!"

"It kind of *is* our fault, though," said George. "If we were gone—"

"If we were gone, he *still* wouldn't be top of the class," Tabitha whispered firmly.

"Yeah, but he'd be closer."

Tabitha snorted. "Does he really think he's going to graduate to year two? He's not ready."

"Is anyone?"

"Actually, rumor has it that Sunny's on the verge of moving up . . . if she aces her midterm. And Ezra, too."

That surprised George. "Ezra? But he's not even in the top five."

"It doesn't matter. Ezra's not so great at the practical stuff, but he's *killing* it in Thieving Theory. They'll probably groom him to be a mastermind behind the scenes, or something." She shook her safe in frustration, like it would magically open for her if she just gave it a good throttle.

"*You* can't move up yet, could you?" George asked.

"I think it's still too soon for me. But maybe by the final exam I'll be ready, if I can *ever open this safe*."

George sighed one enormous breath of relief. It was so nice to have a friend in all his classes. And he was grateful to have someone to study with, especially with the midterm right around the corner.

In fact, Tabitha had already drafted up a study guide for each class, which she'd showed him proudly during breakfast. He knew Tabitha wanted to start studying a little bit each day in the library, where the lighting was so bright it could shrivel eyeballs, but George was hoping to change her mind.

"Hey, what do you think about taking our books into the Robin Hood Room and studying there tonight?"

"With all those fun distractions?" she choked. "Are you cra—"

Strongarm zoomed over to their table and hunched over Tabitha, her back like a boomerang. "TICK!" she shrieked. George put his hands over his ears, but Tabitha didn't blink. She spun to the first number. "TICK!" She reverse-rotated to the second number. "TICK!" She pushed up hard, and spun the lock, looking for the third number. "TICK! TICK!"

CLICK.

The safe opened. Tabitha reached inside eagerly and pulled out—

"*Another* safe?"

The whole class groaned.

"A safe inside a safe inside a safe! Inside a safe, of course!" Strongarm said gleefully. "And whatever you don't finish in class today, you'll do for homework."

The whole class groaned again.

After class, Tabitha dashed off to a Crook Club meeting, and George went straight to the gardens. It was one of those precious September weeks of warm, sunny weather. It seemed like *everyone* was spending time on the grounds before the inevitable cold settled in.

George had taken to sitting under the shade of a brilliantly colored orange tree that faced the gardens, which were still surprisingly in bloom. He'd just pulled out his notebook when Tabitha came running up.

"What are you doing here?" George said, shielding his eyes from the sun as he looked up at her.

She threw down her book bag and plopped next to him. "Crook Club got canceled for today because Ballyrag ate some soured sour cream."

"Ew," George said. "Well, should we do homework, then? We still have those safes to crack."

Surprisingly, Tabitha shook her head.

"Okay, well, should we study for the midterm?" George said. "They're only a week away." Every time George thought about the midterm, his stomach filled with collywobbles.

Many of the older students loved to tell the first-years about the horrors of their own midterms—arrests, broken limbs, dismemberment, and even death. Some fourth-years had told George and Tabitha that only half of their classmates made it back intact—before laughing as they walked away.

Even the teachers tried to scare the first-years. A few of them shouted in the hallways that they always flunked a few students every term for good measure.

George couldn't tell how much was scare tactics, and how much was real. But it frightened him regardless. He and Tabitha now spent almost every evening preparing by poring over books and running practice obstacle courses in the gym. But the worst part about the midterm was that there was no way to prepare because it changed every semester. It could be *anywhere*, stealing *anything*.

And he wasn't the only one running scared. Robin, Neal, Beth, and Becca didn't do anything *but* study anymore. Whenever he ate lunch with them, it was like being in a quiz bowl. Even Milo stayed up into the dead of night, studying silently next to George. But even when they were ten feet away from each other, they still didn't acknowledge the other's existence.

"No midterms, no homework," Tabitha finally said. "Let's just take an hour off!" Using her backpack as a pillow, she lay down and stared up at the clouds.

George did the same.

"Besides," she said, and George could almost hear the grin in her voice, "we have some secret, dastardly plans to concoct. *Muahahahahaha!*"

"What are you talking about?"

"The biggest holiday is right around the corner!"

"Uh . . . Halloween?" George asked.

Tabitha shook her head. "Close. Mischief Night! It's a thief's Christmas."

"Mischief Night . . . that's where people throw toilet paper onto trees and smash pumpkins, right?"

Tabitha snorted. "That's amateur work. We have to come up with something bigger, better, and badder. On Mischief Night, curfew actually gets *canceled* for one night only. We have to do something amaz—"

A rustling noise came from a bush across the garden, and Tabitha cut off mid-word.

George looked over to the sound. "What was—"

"Shhhhh!" she hissed. She slowly began to crawl toward the bush.

WHOOSH!

A stocky boy leaped out from behind the bush and began to sprint toward the school building.

"MILO!" Tabitha shouted after him. "GET BACK HERE! WE SAW YOU! WE *SAW* YOU SPYING ON US!"

"YOU DIDN'T HEAR ANYTHING IMPORTANT, ANYWAY!" George hollered.

When Milo ran through the double doors that led back inside, George and Tabitha sat back down on the grass.

It was the second time George had caught Milo spying on him, and he couldn't help but think that Milo really needed to find a better hobby.

"Milo," Tabitha breathed, her nostrils flaring, "is the *worst*."

Suddenly, George began to laugh and wheeze and snort.

"What?" Tabitha said. "What's so funny?"

"Milo, trying to be all sneaky but getting caught," he snickered.

"Well, it's a good thing I caught him *before* we started talking about our Mischief Night prank. So about that . . ."

They spent the hour brainstorming possible plans, from stealing exhibits to flying Dean Dean Deanbugle's underwear from the ceiling. "Stealing noodles from the kitchen and dropping them all over the stairs!" George proposed. "Eating all of the Triple-dipple Ultra-deluxe Melty Creamy Creamer Rainbow Swizzle Milk Munch ice cream!" Tabitha suggested in reply. They didn't settle on anything, but they had a great list of ideas.

When the sun went down, they packed up and headed to dinner. Rumor was that gourmet mac and cheese was on the menu, and George wanted to be first in line.

But just as they stepped inside the mansion, they ran into Strongarm, wrestling about five chickens in her arms that looked quite intent on flying away from her. In fact, one *did*, flapping across the hall to Tabitha and pecking her braids, like they were some sort of delicious snack.

"Get off me!" Tabitha shrieked, slapping the chicken away.

"Oh, you get back here!" Strongarm hollered at the chicken, as one chicken dug its feet into her hair, and another one nibbled on her ear. "C'mere, chicky chicky chicky! *Squawk! Squawk! Squawwwwwwwwkkkk!*" she squawked.

Tabitha wrestled the chicken and handed it back to Strongarm, though it resisted furiously. "What are the chickens for?" Tabitha asked.

"MIND YOUR OWN BEESWAX!" Strongarm shouted as she scampered off, passing three second-year girls who cowered away from the yawping chickens.

Tabitha tugged on his sleeve. "Mac and cheese, George, remember?"

That got him moving again.

When they got to the dining hall, Tabitha went to get a table, but George ran up to the buffet line so quickly that he accidentally knocked someone face-first into a tray of lobster mac.

It was only when the person stood up again and licked

his face with a long tongue did George realize what he'd done. He froze in horror. "Dean Dean Deanbugle!"

"Cutting the line, I presume?" the dean said, wiping his finger across his face and sticking it in his mouth. His eyebrows were positively caked with cheese. "Well, I can't say that it's even remotely stealthy of you, but I'll give you credit for the theory."

"I'm sorr—" George started, but the disdainful look on the dean's macaronied face stopped him. *That's right—I shouldn't ever apologize.* "I mean, I want what I want, sir, and that mac and cheese is calling my name."

"By all means," Dean Dean Deanbugle said, "take it then."

George marched in front, and he could hear the dean cluck his tongue. "Very good. And by good, I mean bad. And by bad, I mean it's good that you're bad. Very bad, indeed."

The Midterm Exam

On the evening of the exam, George headed down to the Robin Hood Room, which was thankfully empty. He took a dip in the hot tub to relax. Then he doused himself in fancy lotions and oils, jumped on the trampoline to relieve stress, and ate four fluffs of cotton candy just for the fun of it.

He showed up in the foyer just in time to hear the ring of a gong and a chorus of teachers shouting, "ATTENTION! ATTENTION!"

Dean Dean Deanbugle stood by the big double doors—he held up a hand for silence, and the whole hall fell hush. Strongarm and Ballyrag were even holding their hands on their mouths to keep from speaking.

"I will be accompanying you on your midterms!" Dean Dean Deanbugle said. "Now if you would please follow me . . ." He put the big brass key into the keyhole and turned.

George was practically pushed out of the foyer, down the path, and into a yellow school bus. He very quickly regretted eating all that cotton candy, as his stomach was tumbling more than an Olympic gymnast. He wiped his sweaty palms on his pants and tried to think of things that would soothe his nerves. *Kittens! Puppies! Dean Dean Deanbugle's eyebrows!*

"We're ready for this!" Tabitha said, plopping right down next to him. She looked very serious. "We're ready. Hey," she added, squinting at George, "are you okay? You look like you're going to be sick."

George grimaced.

"You're not still thinking about what those fourth-years said, right?" Tabitha said. "I'm sure no one actually dies . . . those fourth-years looked far too happy telling us about it. Plus, none of the older first-years are phased at all."

"I know," he said, feeling a little better.

The bus sputtered and rolled down the hill, and George turned around to look at Pilfer. Sometimes he forgot how beautiful and majestic it was. Especially tonight, where the moonlight was glinting off the exterior vents, making Pilfer Academy look like it was actually sparkling.

When Pilfer disappeared behind them, George faced front. *Don't think of tonight as a test,* he told himself. *Think of tonight as an adventure!* When he thought about it like that, he began to grow excited. He was hitting the open road and ready for a long drive.

But to George's surprise, the bus rolled to a stop just outside a neighborhood twenty minutes away from school.

"Listen up!" said a third-year teacher that George didn't know. "This mission is called: Operation Home Invasion."

"You are to steal a very spatial item!" Ballyrag said. "We've spent months spying on these people with our bunnunculars, and we have discovered each person's most volatile item."

Tabitha cringed. "He means *special*, not spatial! And *valuable*, not volatile."

"You missed *bunnunculars*," George whispered to her, and she elbowed him in response.

"A true thief will show no mercy and no fear!" Browbeat said. "I once stole my own grandfather's gold tooth from his mouth in the middle of the night. If I can do that, you can do *this*."

Ballyrag grunted in agreement.

"And as a special treat, *we* are going to be your Partners in Crime!" Dean Dean Deanbugle said.

Everyone murmured.

"We?" George said. "Who's *we*?"

Tabitha's jaw dropped. "It's the teachers, George! We're partnering with the *teachers*!"

All the students began to buzz about the news.

"Excellent," Milo said loudly, leaning over to George and Tabitha's seat. "Tonight's the night everyone is finally going to see how much better I am than *you*."

Tabitha looked like she could punch Milo.

"You'll *never* be able to beat our scores," George said to him, beneath the sound of Pickapocket trying to shut everyone up. "Not even if we were blindfolded and had our hands tied behind our backs."

"Oh yeah? Where's the rope?" Milo growled.

"Oh, go away, Milo!" Tabitha snapped.

Milo sat back down, but he continued to glower at them during Dean Dean Deanbugle's explanation of the midterm. George ignored him and tried to listen closely to the dean.

The first rule was that they were only allowed off the bus when they were thieving. Otherwise, they were to be guarded by Pickapocket in the front and an upperclassmen teacher in the back.

The thieving, Dean Dean Deanbugle explained, was split into three different shifts. The first round of thieving started at eleven, the second at midnight, and the third at one in the morning. George was part of the second round, assigned to thieve with Strongarm; Tabitha was in the third round with Dean Dean Deanbugle, which—George could tell—made her very nervous, though, to her credit, she wore her nerves with only a grim expression.

"Don't be nervous," George said, though it was probably just as much for his own benefit as Tabitha's.

"I *must* impress Dean Dean Deanbugle," she said, with that hungry, blazing look in her dark eyes. "By the end of this night, he's going to like me even more than he likes you."

George laughed, not quite sure whether she was fully joking, half joking, or not joking at all.

George kept swinging back and forth between fear and excitement. This was his first real test to prove himself. After what the upperclassmen had told him about the midterms, he couldn't help but feel terrified. But a bigger part of him thought that this night would be exhilarating.

He kept impatiently checking his watch every thirty seconds, and it seemed as though time wasn't passing at all. But at long last, at five minutes until midnight, Strongarm came back with Robin, who was waving a gold necklace in the air proudly.

"Killed it!" she said, climbing back onto the bus. "Robin Gold is robbin' gold!"

"Mr. Beckett!" Strongarm beckoned him toward her with a curling finger.

"Good luck!" Tabitha whispered, giving him a quick hug. "See you after!"

"You too," George said, just as Strongarm grabbed him by the wrist and dragged him off the bus.

As he trailed behind Strongarm, a cool wind nipped at his face. George shivered and rubbed his hands together, hoping that the friction would make his hands feel a bit warmer. In the dark, the houses looked nearly identical— with perhaps a small deviation here or there in the style of window shutters or type of front door or placement of shrubberies.

They stopped at a house near the edge of the street, close enough to the bus that he could still see it, but far enough away that he couldn't hear his classmates anymore.

"All right," Strongarm said, "here's your mission: You must steal the brown teddy bear from the two-year-old." She nudged him toward the door. "Go on. Lead the way."

George made his way toward the side door.

"Why not the front door?" Strongarm asked.

"Well, we learned in Thieving Theory that your chance

of the side door being unlocked is about seventy percent more likely than the front door."

Strongarm nodded, her gaunt face looking severe in the moonlight. "Indeed, indeed. Ballyrag has taught you well."

George tiptoed up three wooden steps, and—sure enough—the side door was unlocked. He let himself and Strongarm into the house and shut the door without making so much as a peep.

He found himself in the kitchen of a very dark and gloomy house. Either the family wasn't home or they were asleep, and he paused for a moment to listen for sounds, as he had learned in Browbeat's class. *The key to stealth is patience*, George thought, and he could almost hear it in Browbeat's hoarse voice.

In five minutes of standing there, the only things he heard were the groans of the house, so he finally decided to move forward with the mission. The first thing he noticed was that the wooden floor looked old and creaky, and his footsteps would make much less of a sound if he could muffle them somehow. George looked around the room to see if there was an everyday object he could use as a gadget, and—*aha!* He grabbed two dish towels, put them under his feet, and slid across the hall effortlessly. *Anything can be a gadget*, Pickapocket had said. At last, he reached the carpeted stairs in the foyer. He turned around and tossed the dish towels to Strongarm, who mimicked his every move and caught up to him. George snatched the dish towels and stuffed them in his pocket, just in case he needed to use them later.

He climbed the stairs, and Strongarm silently followed his lead. At the top, George recognized the master bedroom by its double doors, so George turned to the other three bedroom doors. Two were ajar, one was shut—he sneaked closer and popped a head into the two open rooms—one was clearly a guest room, and the other was a half-completed nursery.

That left the closed door.

George gripped the handle, turned, and silently eased the door open. He slid into the room as quietly and slyly as a snake through tall grass. The room was decorated with teddy-bear wallpaper, illuminated by a bear-shaped night-light. He edged to the corner of a large crib and peered in at a toddler, curled up fast asleep. And there— wrapped tightly in the toddler's arms—was the brown teddy bear he needed to steal.

He paused for a moment. He needed to extract the teddy bear from her grip, but first, he needed to think out his escape plan. *Stay three steps in front of the situation*, Ballyrag had said. (Well, really he'd said to stay "affront" of the "salutation," but George knew what he meant.)

Well, there's the window, thought George, *or there's the stairs.* Neither of which made for a completely foolproof exit: windows had a drop and stairs sometimes creaked at unpredictable moments. He knew what he was facing with the stairs, so he slunk to the window and peered out, hoping that there would be a tree he could climb onto or a giant bush that would break his fall.

What he saw was even better—the rooftop sloped underneath the window. He could crawl right onto the roof ledge from that very room—then make his escape by climbing down the drainpipe. He unlatched the windows. Ready. *Prepare before you act,* Strongarm had taught them.

Just in case, he pulled a hand-knit baby blanket off the rocking chair and put it over his head to obscure his face. He peeked out through the holes.

He inched over to the crib, reached in, and gingerly weaseled the teddy bear out of the toddler's grip. She snorted in her sleep, but she didn't wake up, and George breathed a sigh of relief. He went to the window, holding it open as Strongarm squeezed out, then he turned around to climb out feetfirst—

The toddler was standing up in her crib, blinking.

139

Though she was much younger, this toddler instantly reminded him of his little sister, Rosie.

George froze.

"Bear?" she whimpered. "Bear?"

"Shhhhhhhh," George said through the blanket on his head.

"Bear?" she sniffled. She blinked again, and a fat tear rolled down her cheek. She screwed up her face, and George looked behind him. He had to get out of here—fast!

He was one foot out the window when the girl began to wail.

"I WANT BEAR BEAR! MY BEAR BEAR!" she sobbed.

George tightened his grip around the bear. The girl sobbed and blubbered and burbled and hiccupped and screeched.

Guilt twisted his gut. The bear meant so much to the girl, and it meant nothing to him. But he was supposed to steal it, right? It was what his teachers wanted him to do. It was even what his own family thought he'd do, as the Naughty One. This was who he was—who he was supposed to be. A thief. Right?

George bolted with the bear. He snuck out of the window, crawled across the roof, wiggled to the edge, and crawled down using the drainpipe.

Strongarm was waiting for him at the bottom with a wide, dippy grin.

"Excellent, Mr. Beckett. Top form! Exceptional use of gadgets, stealth, theory, and practical applications. With impeccable flair, might I add! And fifteen minutes under the time limit, bravo! But I'll have to deduct a few points for waking up your victim, of course. Now, hand over the bear."

Dazed, George held out the bear, and Strongarm plucked it out of his hands. She led him away from the house's backyard, and as George looked behind him, he saw a light flick on in the toddler's room. He turned back to Strongarm and kept walking, feeling odd.

"You know, if you continue to perform like this, you could move up to year two soon. Of course, I can't make any promises."

George smiled, though it felt like more of a wince.

For the first time in a long time, he thought of his family. He wanted more than anything to talk to his mom or dad about what had just happened. Would the little girl be okay? Did he just do something really wrong? Was it okay to steal something just because an adult told him to?

Strongarm nudged him toward the bus, with Pickapocket huddling by the door like an overly aggressive ostrich.

His classmates all looked up at him curiously, and he knew they were all waiting to hear how it went. "It was awesome," George said as enthusiastically as he could manage.

As he walked the length of the freezing bus, a bit of movement out the window caught his eye—Tabitha was halfway to a house with Dean Dean Deanbugle, so excited she was practically skipping. He must have just missed her.

"Great job, George," Strongarm said. "Next up—Sunny Knight!"

George took his seat, feeling his throat tighten and his ears flush with shame. He hoped no one could tell how he was truly feeling. He huddled by himself, shivering and miserable, but it had nothing to do with the cold.

What to Do

The next morning, George paced around his bedroom. Pale sun peeked through the curtains, making the room's gold trim shimmer. George closed his eyes, knowing that when he opened them, he'd be staring at a stolen comforter on stolen furniture in a stolen house that rightfully belonged to the Duke of Valois.

He looked at all the items that rested on top of his dresser—the silver watch, gold cuff links, leather wallet, and antique alarm clock. And the teddy bear, which Strongarm had given back to him as a trophy. The stupid stuffed bear with its patchy, drool-crusty face glared at him with big glass eyeballs.

George covered it with a baseball hat. But he could still feel its eyes on him, so he covered the hat with a shoebox. Then he covered the shoebox with a lamp shade.

Then he covered the lamp shade with a trash can. After that he felt safe from its judging glass eyes.

"What are you doing?" Milo groaned. "Go back to sleep, Beckett! Or get out."

"Where should I go?"

"Into the whirlyblerg. Feel free to stay there forever." And he collapsed back onto his pillow.

George scurried down to the dining hall, where the waitstaff were setting up a buffet for the second-year, third-year, and fourth-year students, who didn't have an excused late wake-up time. When the doors to the dining hall finally opened for breakfast, George took one look at the buffet and blanched. All of the food in the buffet had been stolen from local restaurants—and he'd been eating it for nearly two months without a care in the world.

He swept out of the dining hall without a bite.

When it finally came time to go to class, he scuffed his feet along the polished floor. He didn't want to go, but he couldn't miss it or he'd meet *severe punishment, frowny-face frowny-face*. And as miserable as he was feeling, he was quite sure that *severe punishment* wouldn't help.

He trudged into Ballyrag's class and took his seat next to Tabitha, who was eager to hear Ballyrag talk about the midterm scores.

She flashed him a grin. "Bet we're still top two," she whispered to him as he sat down.

He returned a feeble smile.

"If we get top scores, let's celebrate with junk food in the Robin Hood Room tonight, okay?" she said, chipper as a chipmunk.

He wasn't remotely in the mood to celebrate, but he nodded anyway.

She stared at him shrewdly. "What's wrong with you? You're so quiet."

Luckily he was spared having to answer her because Ballyrag banged his fist on his desk. "Sunny Kite—get out of my class."

Sunny Knight looked around, confused. "Am I in trouble?"

"You're moving up to year two. You're ready."

The class applauded, but Sunny looked stunned.

"Congratshoelations!" Ballyrag bellowed, taking one of the three shoes he was wearing around his neck and pelting it at her. She squeaked and jumped out of the way before running out of the room.

"She got the bestest score on that exam. And next bestest was . . ." He drummed his hands on his desk. "George Bucket!"

"Beckett," Tabitha whispered automatically, before

squealing and clapping George on the shoulder.

Ballyrag read from a piece of paper. "According to his write-up, Mr. Bucket was unstoppable—he lost points for waking his victim, but he earned points back for being toothless and snatcherling her teddy doll right out of her hands without any desertations. And he got extra points for using a blanket as a sneakery disguise. He is our newest most accomplerished thief, and we are proud of his pecatcular display of criminalism."

Ballyrag applauded, and the class joined in, his friends loudest of all. Milo folded his arms and sneered. Then, Ballyrag moved on to complimenting the third highest score, which was Tabitha. But George barely listened as he sunk down in his desk.

Ballyrag's praise echoed around in his head. His teachers were so proud of him, but why did every compliment feel like a knife in his navel?

He exhaled deeply. What was wrong with him? It wasn't like he didn't know he was attending thieving school. He had never had a problem with the thieving part before, so he couldn't possibly understand what had changed.

"You did *great!*" Tabitha hissed to him as Ballyrag proceeded to reprimand Tosh and Carrie on nearly getting caught. "What's the matter?"

"Nothing," George said quietly.

He couldn't concentrate all day long—he tripped into a pile of mice while running drills during Strongarm's class. In Browbeat's class, he bungled his Irish accent so badly that he sounded like he was from Brooklyn. And when Pickapocket asked what a thief could do with a blanket, George answered, "Take a nap." Pickapocket spent the remaining ten minutes of class shrieking at him, to Milo's obvious delight.

After class, he told Tabitha that he'd meet her in the Robin Hood Room after he changed—but that was a lie. The Robin Hood Room had lost its charm.

He wandered the hall, his stomach growling. He hadn't eaten anything all day, and now everyone he passed looked like a walking, talking chicken nugget. He stood against the wall, watching the giant chicken nuggets talk to one another.

"Yum, yum, yum! I am delicious!" said a third-year chicken nugget.

"Food is so tasty! Sooooo tastyyyyyy," replied a year-two chicken nugget.

"Uh, George?" Beth said as she passed by him. She smelled like chicken nuggets. "You've got a little drool on your . . . well, everywhere."

He blushed and wiped his mouth with his sleeve. Then

he ran to the dining hall to find some chicken nuggets. As much as he hated eating stolen food, he couldn't go on starving himself any longer.

George ate so much that he felt like he was going to burst. Then he spent the rest of the night prowling around corners, avoiding everyone before finally falling asleep ridiculously early.

For days, he wandered the hallways, wishing his stomach didn't feel like it was worming its way through a ropes course. The more he thought about the midterm, the more flushed he became—until he was so certain he was developing a fever that he paced outside the infirmary. The only reason he was able to talk himself out of going in was because Nurse Embezzle loved to poke people with her knee plexor—not just in the knees but all over the body to test reaction times. Being repeatedly whacked in the gut sounded like the opposite of what George needed right now.

He was more irritable than he'd ever been at Pilfer, and he wanted nothing more than to be left alone. After the fourth day in a row of dashing away from Tabitha the moment she suggested they do anything, he found himself on the rooftop terrace, watching the twilight sun brighten the autumn leaves in a blanket of solid gold. It was the only type of gold he was certain Pilfer Academy wouldn't try to steal.

Maybe.

A gust of wind smacked him in the face, and he peeled away from the wall, only to find Tabitha standing right behind him.

"Why are you avoiding me?"

"I'm not avoiding you."

Tabitha shook her head. "I know Browbeat's stealth tactics when I see them." She walked over to the balcony and leaned out. "Are you going to tell me what's wrong, or do I have to guess?"

George sighed and stared pointedly at the ground.

"What's wrong, George?" Tabitha insisted.

"It's nothing."

"George," she said, putting a hand on his shoulder. "We're best friends—you can talk to me. Maybe I can help."

George squinted. Setting sunlight shined on Pilfer's exterior vents, and the glare was getting in his eyes. "Fine . . . It's about the midterm. I stole a toddler's teddy bear, and I—I feel really bad about it."

Tabitha scrunched her nose. "George, if Browbeat doesn't feel bad about stealing his grandfather's gold tooth, then you shouldn't feel bad about stealing a dumb teddy bear. You can't break down every time you steal something."

"Maybe it's a sign that I shouldn't be stealing things."

Tabitha's dark eyes bulged until they were practically popping out of her head.

"Maybe," George whispered, "I'm not cut out for this."

Now that the sun was fully gone and there was not much left to see anymore, George wandered over to a bench in the middle of the terrace and sat down. But Tabitha continued to lean against the balcony as she stared disbelievingly at him.

"What, do you want to leave Pilfer or something, George?" she joked.

"I—I don't know. Maybe," he said, looking down at his feet. "Yes," he added softly.

Tabitha looked like she was going to faint. Or explode. Or both. "*WHAT?*" she shrilled. "But what? Why? George, you're *good* at stealing! And this is the best school for thieves! You're ranked number two! You have a key! And teachers who believe in you, and lessons that teach you the most amazing things . . ." She continued to chatter about the benefits of a Pilfer education, but George was barely listening.

Once he'd said the truth out loud, George knew there was no taking it back: He didn't want to be here anymore. He was no thief. He didn't belong at Pilfer Academy.

The Woeful Tale of Reuben Odell

Saturdays were usually lazy days. With no classes to attend, the hallways were deserted in the mornings, and students didn't usually roll out of bed until 1:00 p.m., at least. This morning was no different. George shuffled around from room to room, wandering aimlessly.

He felt bad that he had been avoiding Tabitha, and felt even worse when she'd begged him to stay at Pilfer. And even worse still when, after she didn't change his mind, she stormed off in a huff.

He wasn't sure why Tabitha didn't understand how he felt. The more he went over what happened, the more he remembered what she'd said: *What, do you want to leave Pilfer or something, George?*

It was a thought.

A fascinating thought.

What if he *could* leave Pilfer? Escape was not an option, right? Or was it? Could he steal Dean Dean Deanbugle's big brass key, the one that he used to unlock the front door during their midterm exam? Or there were the fourth-years, who were almost always off campus, completing their thesis projects. They had special keys that led to a secret exit . . . perhaps he could steal one of those.

These thoughts ran through his head constantly, filling him with hope. And despite everything, there was just one person he wanted to share that feeling with. After a half hour of wandering Pilfer, George found Tabitha in a study room in the Sundance Kid Wing.

"There you are!" George said, shutting the door behind him. "I've been looking all over for you."

"Yes?" she said stiffly.

"I'm sorry," George said. He didn't know what he was sorry for, but he felt like that's what Tabitha wanted him to say.

She kicked out a chair for him, and he took it.

"I'm just brainstorming for our disguise project for Browbeat," she said. "Do you think I could pull off fake sideburns? Have you started yours yet?"

"No. I've been thinking more."

"About?"

"Tabitha—what if I escaped?"

She looked down at her homework and scribbled. "You can't escape," she said, keeping her voice low. She tiptoed to the window of the study room and looked out in the hall.

George looked, too, but he couldn't see anyone lurking—or even passing by. He closed the blinds, just to be safe. "Sure I can," he continued in a whisper. "I could steal Dean Dean Deanbugle's key. Or climb the wall outside. Or dig a hole underneath—"

"No, I mean, you *won't* escape."

"What do you mean? Why not?"

Her eyes darted to the study room window again, but there wasn't anything to see with the blinds down. "Have you ever heard of Reuben Odell?"

"Reuben O Who?"

"Reuben Odell. He's practically a Pilfer legend."

George shrugged, and Tabitha continued.

"Reuben was a fourth-year many years ago, and while he was off campus for his thesis project, he called the police on Pilfer."

"Called the *police*? What—why—how? What happened?"

"Well, at first the police just laughed at him, but eventually he got them to check it out. So they came to Pilfer—"

"Did they get inside?"

"Dean Dean Deanbugle greeted them at the door, and he ended up convincing them that it was a prank from a student who was very homesick. And the police believed him."

"Because Reuben's story was too ridiculous?"

"That," Tabitha nodded, "but also because Dean Dean Deanbugle knows how to manipulate the police. I mean, there's that third-year class *How to Manipulate the Police*."

George looked up at Tabitha, who stared back at him with a grim expression. He'd come into the study room so hopeful and happy—now he only felt nauseous. "So what happened?" he finally asked, unsure whether he actually wanted to hear the rest of the story.

"Dean Dean Deanbugle had to move the school. I mean, just think of how suspicious it would have looked if the police received just one more phone call. So they moved the mansion to a different town, across the country."

"Ha-ha, very funny. No, really, what happened?"

Tabitha blinked. "Were you not listening? *They had to move the school.*"

"Move the school?" George said. "But how? That's . . . that's impossible! How do you move a whole building?"

"Pilfer's easily movable—you've seen the metal vents on the side of the building, right?"

George nodded. "Yeah—Strongarm told me they were a last resort."

"Well, I don't know how it works exactly, but I overheard some other students talking about it once, and I think that's part of how it moves. Pilfer has a perfect getaway if we need it, but it's much less hassle to stay put. They'll do whatever they can to keep their students'— and former students'—lips sealed."

"And Reuben?" George was almost afraid to ask.

"Whirlyblerg," Tabitha said grimly.

"And after that?"

"I don't think you understand—there *is* no after when it comes to the whirlyblerg. No one's heard from Reuben since."

"Since when?"

"I don't know." Tabitha twirled one of her braids between her fingers and sighed. "The point is—you can't tell anyone about Pilfer, and you *can't* escape. If they think you're a threat to the school, then you're in big trouble."

George let out a shaky, nervous chuckle. "Are you sure this is even a real story? It sounds made up to me."

"I swear it's true," Tabitha said firmly. "Every word. If you don't believe me, ask the fourth-years. Some of them were here when it happened. Or ask the waitstaff—I bet they'll remember."

"I will," George said. "Right now."

And with his mission in mind, he marched to the dining hall. Many of the waitstaff were pretty old—teenagers, or maybe just a bit older than that. And a few were *really, really* dinosaurically old, like his parents' age.

He caught eyes with a balding waiter.

George waved him over, and the waiter came running. "Can I get you something, young sir?" the waiter said to him. "A glass of orange juice perhaps?"

"No, thank you," George said. "But can I ask you a question?"

"Of course, young master."

"Have you ever heard of Reuben Odell?"

The man jumped. "I—I—this is most indecent to discuss, sir!" he squeaked. "Good day!"

The man bolted toward the staff door.

"Wait!" George shouted, throwing his chair behind him. "Come back!"

The waiter scurried to the left, then to the right, hopping about like a jackrabbit.

There were a few students in the room, curiously watching George chase after a waiter, but he didn't have time to think about them. He sprinted as fast as he could and jumped onto the waiter, like he was getting a free piggyback ride. "HA! GOTCHYA!" George said, wrapping his legs around him. Then dropping his voice, he hissed, "What do you know about Reuben Odell? Is it true he got sent to the whirlyblerg for trying to escape?"

"I am not at liberty to discuss."

"Aha! So you *do* know something."

The waiter looked furious with himself.

"I know nothing," the waiter said.

George's grip was slipping, so he slid off the waiter's back and held on tight to his blazer. "Did Reuben really try to escape? Is he still in the whirlyblerg?"

"I said I know nothing!" the waiter squeaked, and he wiggled out of the jacket George clung to—leaving him free to make his escape.

The waiter scampered into the kitchen and out of sight. George tried to follow him through the door to the kitchen, but it was locked. When he turned around, all the other waitstaff seemed to have disappeared from the dining hall, and that was the end of that.

The Lie Detector Test

George didn't know what to do. Tabitha was acting distant and sour. And he felt like he didn't have much in common with Robin, Neal, Beth, and Becca anymore. All they wanted to talk about was their plans for Mischief Night, but that was the *last* thing George wanted to talk about. The thought of being forced to participate in any more thieving made him want to throw up.

But he couldn't avoid it. Now that midterms were over, the whole school was abuzz with talk of Mischief Night, just a month away. The teachers had started to make formal announcements about how curfew was canceled for the whole night and explaining the rules (there were none). And thanks to Milo, George couldn't even escape Mischief Night in his own room: Milo had starting nicking supplies from around school and was storing them in boxes on their floor.

All the Mischief Night mania was starting to make George feel a bit desperate . . . like he would do *anything* to be gone by then.

He was so distracted by thoughts of escape that he hardly listened to Ballyrag's lecture on fear tactics, which he called *fear taxes*. Before he knew it, there was going to be a quiz the next day on material George hadn't even bothered to listen to.

The weird thing was that he still felt like he needed to pass. If he started failing, then he might be picked to be part of the waitstaff—or *worse*, sent to the whirlyblerg— and then there would be no chance of leaving.

So at dinner he vowed to learn the material from Robin, Beth, and Becca, who had very graciously offered to tutor him.

"So what's the whole point of fear tactics again?" he asked.

"You can bend your victim to your will much more easily if he's running scared," Becca said. "You have to set the tone for intimidation . . . or something like that."

"And how do I intimidate?"

"Threat and scream. That's your power stance," Beth said.

"And for extra credit: punching inanimate objects," Robin said cheerily. "That is always frightening."

"Mmmm," George said, swallowing a bite of his veal Parmesan. He saw a waitress and tried to wave her over, but she squeaked and ran in the other direction. It was like that with all the waitstaff now; they refused to even *look* at him. It was making mealtimes very awkward.

"Hey, George!" Robin said, snapping in front of his face. He turned his attention back to her.

"Sorry," he said.

"I just asked if you had any more questions."

George nodded. "What was Ballyrag saying about nativity again?"

"He meant creativity," Beth said. "At least . . . I think."

"The point," Becca answered, "is that you have to get creative with your fear tactics. People have seen too many movies and read too many books. They're not getting as frightened as they used to be, so you have to think outside the box to really scare—"

"Hey!" shouted someone from across the hall.

George looked up. Neal was walking over to his table, holding a note. "Dean Dean Deanbugle wants to see you."

"Me?" George said.

"Yeah," Neal said, flicking the note to George.

My office. Now. P.S. Bring a tray of stroganoff with you.

"Am I in trouble?" George said.

"Yeah." Neal laughed, wiggling his fingers. "Beware the whirlyblerg!"

George swallowed the lump in his throat and tried not to think of the whirlyblerg as he piled up a plate of beef stroganoff for the dean. When George headed upstairs and knocked on the dean's bookcase, the door immediately swiveled around. The dean's face fell when he saw the plate of stroganoff George was carrying.

"What, just a plate? I asked for a *tray!*"

"I'm sorry, Dean Dean Deanbugle! I . . . could go back and get you more if you want."

The dean snatched the plate from George and retreated into his office. George took a seat in one of the big plushy chairs.

Dean Dean Deanbugle leaned over his desk. He stared at George. George stared back. He stared harder. George stared even harder than that. Neither blinked. Both squinted.

At last, eyes burning, George blinked.

"Ha-HA!" Dean Dean Deanbugle shouted. "I win!"

"Oh . . . uh. . . . Congrats?"

Dean Dean Deanbugle nodded grimly, and his eyebrows suddenly dipped so low they nearly covered his eyes—like a nice, hairy blanket. "I suppose you're wondering why I brought you in here."

George nodded.

"Well, first, I was dying for a taste of that stroga-noff." Using his hand like a ladle, Dean Dean Deanbugle scooped a fistful of noodles into his palm, brought it to his lips, and slurped. "But second, I had some questions to ask you. Ready?"

"Sure?"

"What's your name?"

"George."

"Your full name?"

"George Beckett."

"Your full full name?"

"George Gilbert Beckett."

"What is your ultimate thieving goal?"

"To . . . uh . . . steal the Eiffel Tower?"

"Do you enjoy Pilfer Academy of Filching Arts (We Steal Things)?"

George's heart did a little kick. "Yes, of course," he lied.

"Now complete this sentence: Peter Piper picked a peck of pickled . . ."

"Pickles?"

"Peppers."

"Peppers?"

"A peck of pickled peppers Peter Piper picked."

George scratched his head. "Uh . . . What are we talking about, sir?"

The dean smiled. "This is a human lie detector test."

"But . . . but you haven't put any wires on me. And you're not even holding my wrists to feel a pulse."

"Oh, I can determine the truth with my brain alone."

"Well . . . what's this all about?"

"You'll never guess what happened to me just two days ago," Dean Dean Deanbugle said. "Go on. Guess."

"I don't know, sir."

"Guess!"

"I really have no idea—"

"Guessssssssss!" the dean whined.

"You stole something?"

"Wrong! I ate a plate of the most delicious macaroni I've ever had. But you'll never guess what happened yesterday."

"You had another plate of macaroni?"

"No! Well, yes! Yes, I did. But *also*, a student told me yesterday that you wished to leave Pilfer, George . . . so I decided to find out whether there was any truth to this matter, or whether this was a normal bout of academic envy."

"But . . . who?"

"Someone very close to you," Dean Dean Deanbugle

said, slurping up some stroganoff. He got gravy all over his chin, but he did absolutely nothing to wipe it up. "In fact, you might even say that you and this person are . . . thick as thieves!" The dean paused to slap his knee. "Get it? *Get it?*"

George smiled weakly, but a stab of betrayal hit him in the gut. It had to be Tabitha—she was the only one who knew what he was really feeling. But how could she double-cross him like that?

"But I've determined that there is nothing to this rumor. You've passed the lie detector test."

"That's . . . that's great," George hesitated.

But Dean Dean Deanbugle didn't notice—as he stood up and bent over, his back arched like a wishbone. He stuck his face close to the plate, pointed his long tongue, and began licking the plate clean like a cat. Finally, when there was nothing but saliva left, the dean stood up, wiped his mouth with his sleeve, and said, "Deeeeeelicious. But next time, do bring that tray. Or I'll send you to the whirlyblerg!"

George winced.

"Don't worry, George," the dean continued. "This false, malicious rumor didn't taint my opinion of you. You are still my protégé, my favorite student, the crème de la crème of this institution. You know who you remind me of?"

"You, sir?"

"No! Of course not! I'm the only me special enough to remind me of me! But you, George, remind me of Sir Nicolas Hurtsalot, my very first favorite pupil. Very accomplished thief, never been caught. Very famous among the thieving world for stealing the president's underpants. During a live speech, no less." Dean Dean Deanbugle took a deep breath. "I'm so glad that there's no truth to this most disgraceful rumor. You have a good day now, George."

George stood up and made his way to the door, trying to ignore Dean Dean Deanbugle chanting behind him:

"Whirlyblerg spin!
Whirlyblerg fly!
Just throw them in the whirlyblerg
And say good-bye!"

Friendship Over

As soon as he was back in the grand marble hall, George lost his cool.

He raged through the school. It *had* to be Tabitha. She was the only person he told. Was this why she was so cold lately? Did she feel so guilty that she couldn't face him? Could they go from being best friends one moment to nothing the next? Maybe he was just deluding himself into thinking they were really friends after all.

He rounded a corner and ran smack into Milo.

"OW!" they both said together, rubbing their shoulders where they'd collided.

"GEORGE!" Milo snarled. "You—you're trying to break my leg aren't you?" Milo's eyes widened, and then he began kicking and smashing his leg against the wall.

"What are you *doing*?!" George cried.

"HELP! TEACHERS! COME QUICK! GEORGE IS BREAKING MY LEG!"

"What! No I'm not! You're breaking your *own* leg!"

Milo grinned wickedly. "Now I got you! COME QUICK! SOMEONE!" he yelled again, now punching his leg with his fists.

"I—I don't have time for this!" George said, brushing past him and sprinting away from the scene of the bizarre self-inflicted crime.

George went back to searching for Tabitha, and he knew exactly where Tabitha would be after 8:00 p.m. on a Tuesday. He stormed into the library and, sure enough, she was in her usual study chair beneath a sign that read:

SHHHH! THIS IS A LIBRARY!
IF I HEAR YOU TALKING, I'LL SNATCH YOUR BAG.
BECAUSE THAT'S WHAT I DO.
—Bagsnatcher

"Did you think I wouldn't find out?" he said quietly.

Tabitha looked up, startled.

"Find out what?" she said, quieter than quietly.

"That you went to Dean Dean Deanbugle?" he said, quieter than quieter than quietly.

"I did *what*?" she breathed.

167

"You—you went to him—making up rumors about me. Lying to him about . . . about stuff," he muttered.

"I haven't the foggiest idea what you're talking about," she uttered, retreating back behind her book.

George pulled the book out of her hands. "You said we were friends," he sighed.

"Friends?" she grumbled. "Oh, like you've been a good one of *those* lately."

"Well, I guess we're not friends anymore," George hushed.

Tabitha stood up, tears in her eyes. "Fine," she hissed.

"Fine," he whispered.

"Fine," she mouthed.

George was determined to get the last murmur, but the librarian, Bagsnatcher, waddled over to their table. "I daresay, can you fight a little louder?"

Tabitha's eyebrows knit together. "But this is a library!"

"Of course," Bagsnatcher said. "Which means that everyone's doing lots of boring work, studying very hard, and having absolutely no fun. We could all use a good distraction." She reached into her pocket, pulled out a plastic bag full of popcorn, and began munching loudly, watching them with interest.

Nothing breaks up a private fight like a public audience, and so George turned on his heels and marched into the hall, to the boos and hisses of his classmates who were hoping to witness a brawl.

George replayed their fight over and over in his head, and he kept feeling sicker and sicker about it as the day wore on. Could their friendship really be over?

At night, he lay on his bed for hours. He had a miserable sleep, twisting and turning under his covers, unable to shut off his brain. He was thankful when dawn broke, so he could put on his slippers and take a stroll around the mansion.

Room by room, he ambled around, looking at the plaques that detailed what each exhibit was, who it was taken from, and when it was taken. He knew the mansion was big, but it was the first time he realized how *enormous* it really was—and how many generations' worth of things had been stolen in the name of Pilfer Academy.

He was alone in his wanderings until he hit the first floor. Crossing in front of the Robin Hood Room was Robin Gold in her pajamas.

"Early morning stroll?" George said.

She smiled brightly. "Actually," she said, looking around to make sure no one else was in the hall, "I just woke up on a foam pit. I guess I sleepwalked into the Robin Hood Room last night. . . ."

"Lucky you didn't get caught!" George said.

"Even my sleepwalks are sneaky! Why are you out here? Are you okay? I haven't seen anyone this glum since my great-aunt Gertrude choked on a finger sandwich."

George sighed.

"I wish you two would stop fighting already," Robin said. "Tabitha is really upset. She keeps crying at night. She thinks I don't hear her, but I do."

He didn't know what to say, so he didn't say anything.

"You know how much your friendship means to her, right?"

George wasn't sure it meant *anything* to her. He folded his arms stubbornly.

"Anyway, you should just go talk to her," Robin insisted, and she scurried away.

All day, George tried not to look at Tabitha in class, but he found that he couldn't stop glancing at her. And the more he glanced at her, the more he thought about how mad he was. How hurt he was. How betrayed he felt.

How their friendship was over.

But there was one good thing that came out of this: Their fight was the final push he needed. Because now that he'd lost Tabitha, there was nothing keeping him at Pilfer anymore.

Failures for All!

George spent the next two weeks coming up with different escape plans in his head. (He didn't dare write anything down, just in case someone stole the incriminating evidence.) By the end of the second week, he had many options:

1. Dig a tunnel under the wall

2. Climb the wall

3. Steal Dean Dean Deanbugle's key to the school

4. Get a fourth-year to let him out, using one of their special swipe cards at the secret exit

5. Swipe the fighter plane from the lobby, find some gas, and fly it out of here

6. Steal the trampoline from the Robin Hood Room and use it to jump over the wall

7. Find where they're keeping the ice-cream trucks and drive home

8. Let the exotic bugs exhibit loose inside the school, and escape as the exterminator is let in

He had a zillion other plans, too, but the problem with all these ideas was that he had no idea where Pilfer was—or what to do once he escaped. How would he get home? And what would stop his teachers from coming after him? They had been watching him for a long time before they kidnapped him, so they knew where he lived, who his family was, and how to find him. They could just drag him back by his toes and toss him in the whirlyblerg for trying to escape, and there would be nothing he could do about it.

So he pondered and pondered and pondered some more. After his last class that Friday, George sat down on a couch in the Blackbeard Wing to mull over his options again with a decoy schoolbook on his lap.

What sort of escape plot would let him go home permanently? How could he avoid being forced to participate in this school? Or worse, sent to the whirlyblerg?

He stared at the pages, thinking.

"Homework on a Friday afternoon?" said a voice

behind him. George whipped around to find Strongarm beaming. "I fought for your admission, you know. Some of the other teachers wanted to choose this gymnast girl because of her double-back-handspring-back-tuck. Impressive, indeed, but you are much more sneakerific."

"Sneakerific?"

"It's Ballyrag's new word for when someone is sneak-tastic. Or maybe he was talking about his collection of sneakers . . . it's hard to tell sometimes."

George nodded. *It's funny,* he thought, *that Strongarm thinks I'm working so hard on my homework. If only she knew I was plotting my escape!*

"Don't expect too much from my next homework assignment," George said. "I'm . . . erm . . . having a tough time with this new material."

"Do you need extra tutoring? Where's your partner in crime—Miss Tabitha Crawford? Maybe she could help you. We wouldn't want you to fail out now, would we?"

"Fail out?" he wheezed, thinking only of the miserable expression on every single waiter's face. "But—I—how—"

"Oh, dear boy, I'm just kidding!" Strongarm cackled. "You won't fail out! Of that, I am certain."

George breathed a sigh of relief.

"Everyone at this school is the best of the best,"

Strongarm reminded him. "And if someone's not good at theory or stealth, you can bet they'll be good at *some* specialty. Why, just before you got here, we moved up a boy from second to third year. He was failing every class— but he is the best pickpocket this school has ever seen!"

George hesitated. They were tap-dancing around the topic—right on a razor's edge of the truth—and he knew this was his chance to get some *real* information, if he just asked the right things. "So . . ." he said cautiously. "What about the waitstaff? Weren't they once the best of the best, too?"

Strongarm sucked in a sharp breath. "I don't believe this conversation is appropriate, George. You won't fail out, I assure you—"

"Please," George said, and he sniveled into a tissue for dramatic effect, which was a manipulation trick he'd picked up from Ballyrag's class. "A third-year told me that I'll become part of the waitstaff if I don't have a good prank for Mischief Night," he lied. "I'm so very scared!"

"Poppycock! Codswallop! Twaddle! Claptrap! Drivel! Rubbish! Tosh! Tripe! Baloney! Bunkum!"

"Are . . . are you okay?" George interrupted.

"Here's the truth of the matter, George, and don't you go telling anyone I told you this." She looked around frantically and dropped her voice to a very loud whisper.

"The people who fail here fail because they want to fail."

"Huh?"

"If you give up, you fail. If you don't want to try, you fail. If your heart's not in it . . ."

George's stomach walloped.

"But," Strongarm said, "if you try, try, try, then you'll move up to the next level in anywhere from a few months to about seven years." She cleared her throat. "Ah, maybe I shouldn't have said anything. Now you'll think this school's too easy."

"I don't think it's easy at all," George said quietly, but Strongarm didn't hear him as she began shouting, "FAIL-URES FOR ALL! YOU FAIL AND YOU FAIL AND YOU FAIL! EVERYONE FAILS!"

She ran down the hallway, and for minutes after, George could hear her shouting, "FAILURE!" at students.

Now he knew: He had to prove to them that he still wanted to be here. But somehow make *them* not want him. And there was only one way to do that.

He had to get expelled.

My Best Work... Honest!

George got to work right away by completing his homework entirely, 100 percent wrong.

But the real work began once the weekend was over. On Monday morning, he had an exam in Thieving Theory.

"G'luck," Ballyrag said, plopping the test paper in front of George.

Question 1: How would you break into a building with heavy security?

I would walk right in. If any guards tried to stop me, I would sing to distract them. Once inside, I would bribe everyone with string cheese to keep quiet about all this. Also, I must introduce myself, so that I become the most FAMOUS SUPER THIEF IN ALL THE WORLD.

George smiled to himself. That would *surely* get him an F.

Question 2: What is the acronym you must remember for when a situation gets out of hand?

George knew the real answer was *RASH:* Run And Stay Hidden. But instead he wrote:

STATE

Stay

There

And

Tickle

Everyone

By the end of the test, George was sure that he had failed just enough to make it seem like he wasn't cut out for thievery.

When the bell rang, George handed in his exam, and followed his classmates toward Practical Applications of Breaking and Entering—when someone patted him on the shoulder.

"How'd you do, George?" Neal asked.

"Oh, um, all right I think."

"I thought the test went awesomely. I think I'm a shoe-in for a key next time rankings come out."

"I'm sure you are," George said sincerely, thinking that Neal would probably have *his* key.

"Yeah, I've been struggling with Thieving Theory, but luckily Robin has been tutoring me. We studied like *crazy* this weekend. I must have aced—"

They walked into the big ballroom, to find a set of extra tall monkey bars set up. Beneath the monkey bars was an inflatable pool, filled to the brim with creamed spinach. Strongarm stood next to the monkey bars, wiggling her arms excitedly as she waited for them all to file in.

"What's this?" Adam called out.

"THE MONKEY BARS OF DOOM!" Strongarm shouted gleefully. "You have to get across all the monkey bars to pass. If you fall into the spinach, it's an automatic delicious snack. Now who would like to try their luck?"

George raised his hand quickly . . . even quicker than Tabitha.

"George!" Strongarm said. "I saw you first! Come on up!"

George walked up to the ladder and climbed up. Everyone was silent except for Strongarm, who was giggling madly.

When he got to the top, George put his hand on the first bar to start traveling across, but his hand slid right off. "What the—" He tried again, but it slipped again. There was no way to grip the monkey bars.

"I'VE BUTTERED THEM!" Strongarm cackled. "AND OILED THEM! Why, I've OTTERED—NO, NO! I'VE BOILED THEM! That's the combination between buttered and oiled, you know."

George was hardly paying attention to her.

If he were doing this obstacle course for real, then he'd climb up on top of the monkey bars—so that they were below him—and crawl across. But he had to make himself try and fail.

He wrapped his arms, pretzel-knot style, around the first bar and clung to it. Then, with a deep breath, he uncurled one of his arms and reached for the next one—

SSSLLLLLIIIIIPPPPPPP!

As expected, he slid straight off the monkey bars and landed with a *SQUISH!* in the creamed spinach.

There was creamed spinach *everywhere*. In his eyes, in his ears, up his nose, under his shirt, in his socks— he felt like a spinach monster.

Strongarm guffawed, pointing and laughing. "NOW YOU HAVE TO LICK YOURSELF OFF!" she roared.

"HA-HA! FAILURE!" Milo shouted with glee.

George spent the rest of the day with creamed spinach caked all over him. Which eventually hardened and formed a smelly protective shell. George was not allowed to shower until after classes were over ("THIS IS YOUR PUBLIC SHAME!" Strongarm had shouted to the people who'd failed the trial.), but the second the day ended, he spent two hours in the bathroom, scrubbing himself free.

After five straight days of Plan Failing-on-Purpose-but-Making-It-Look-Like-an-Accident, George felt no closer to being expelled than he was a week ago. The only real difference was that he was a lot more banged and bruised.

On Friday, he was ready to accept defeat—until Dean Dean Deanbugle walked into his Stealth Class. *This is my big chance!* George thought. He couldn't mess up . . . which was to say that he *had* to mess up.

The class got very stiff when the dean burst in.

"Don't mind me," Dean Dean Deanbugle said, his eyebrows dancing a jig. "I'll just observe in the back!" He sat on a table in the back of the classroom, reached into his pocket, and pulled out a cup full of linguini. He twirled the pasta around his fingers, held his hand above his mouth, and then sucked his fingers clean.

"Right," Browbeat said, adjusting his oversized glasses. "Like I was saying, today we are going to practice sneaking down a hallway. Dean Dean Deanbugle and I are going to sit on either end of the hall, and if we can't hear you slinking down it, you pass."

They followed Browbeat to a hallway, all set up with special booby traps. There was a piano mat, bubble wrap, plastic bags, crunchy leaves from outside, and a few puddles. The hallway looked like a wreck, but a fun one.

Milo went first and made just one sigh of relief when he narrowly avoided a collision with a coatrack. Points were deducted, but he still passed. Tabitha passed with flying colors—and record time. About five other classmates went, and then it was George's turn.

He started slinking along the side of the wall, thinking about how he could make the most damage—when he saw the perfect opportunity.

He pretended to trip over his own two feet and went headfirst into a metal trash bin.

CRASH! The trash bin rolled into a bike. *CLATTER!* The bike fell onto a cardboard box. *CRUNCH!* Inside the box was a sleeping cat. *HISS!* The cat ran across the piano mat. *DUM DUM DUM DUMMMM!*

George froze on the spot, as Browbeat and Dean Dean Deanbugle turned around to glare at him.

"Ooops!" George said. "I guess I'm not so great at this! Clumsy me!"

"George," Browbeat grumbled, wiping his glasses with his sleeve. "That's the fifth day in a row you've fallen short of expectations—not just in my class, but in your other teachers' classes."

Dean Dean Deanbugle wiggled his furry eyebrows. "Is this *true?*"

"We've discussed it in the teachers' lounge, yes," Browbeat said. "It was our most gossipy piece of gossip."

"George," Dean Dean Deanbugle said as he reached into his sleeve, pulled out one single linguini strand, and slurped it ominously, "what do you have to say for yourself?"

George's stomach flopped, but he had to stick to the plan. "I'm trying my hardest!"

The dean hung over him like a gnarled umbrella. "You claim this is the best you can do? Is that your final answer?"

"I—I—maybe I just don't have a talent for this stuff?" George added in a small voice.

"Then we have a huge problem." Dean Dean Deanbugle plucked him off the ground and popped him over his shoulder. George thrashed and fought and squirmed, but Dean Dean Deanbugle carried him as easily as if he were a kitten.

As he was being carted away, George saw his classmates gawking and Milo grinning, but all too soon George and the dean rounded a corner.

Then George was alone.

And in deep trouble.

The Whirlyblerg

"Where are you taking me?" George asked, trying to keep his voice from wobbling.

The dean continued to carry him over his shoulder. George rode down the hall, through a door, and down some very winding stairs.

"I'm doing this for your own good, George."

"Doing what?"

"You had talent last week, now this week you don't. We only have the best of the best here at Pilfer, so . . ."

George's heart leaped. This was the part where Dean Dean Deanbugle was going to tell him that he was expelled. That they were going to give up on him.

"So," the dean said, "we just have to shake the talent back *in* to you."

George hung like a wet noodle over the dean's shoulder. "Shake?" he whispered.

"THE WHIRLYBLERG!" Dean Dean Deanbugle confirmed.

George felt like he was going to be sick. He began to thrash again, but Dean Dean Deanbugle said, "Oh no you don't! I've wrestled students twice your size into the whirlyblerg *and* students half your size—which are a lot trickier as there's less of them to hold on to. Slippery little things."

"But I haven't done anything wrong!" George said. "HELP HELP HELP!!!"

But he knew his screaming *wouldn't* help, as Dean Dean Deanbugle was dragging him through a dark, drippy hallway. They must have been underground—that was the only thing that would explain the lack of windows and lights. The only lights came from the rotted Jack-o-lanterns that lined the hall.

George sniffed, and instantly regretted it. "UGH! What's that smell?"

"We keep meaning to replace the pumpkins . . ." Dean Dean Deanbugle said. "They were carved about seven years ago. It's just that we so rarely come down here that we keep forgetting."

"The candles inside haven't blown out?"

"They're battery oper—"

"HELPPPPPPPPPPPP!!!!!!" George shouted, figuring it was worth another try. He pounded his hands on Dean Dean Deanbugle's back. "HELPPPPPPPPP HEEEEEELLLLLPPPP!! SOMEBODY HELP ME, PLEAS-EEEEEEEE!!!!!!!!"

His words echoed around the empty hallway.

Dean Dean Deanbugle gripped him tighter. "You see why I have to do this, George. I'm punishing you because I care."

For a moment, George thought how utterly twisted that was, but then he lost that thought—and his breath—as they approached a big door. Fear gripped his chest; on the door, there was a sign that read:

DANGER ZONE:
THIS WAY FOR ~~TORTURE~~ FUN FUN FUN!

Dean Dean Deanbugle kicked open the door, and they were inside. The room was bright and big—with rainbow-painted walls and happy music blaring from the speakers.

And smack dab in the middle of the room was a carnival ride with kids and adults of all ages strapped in.

It was a music express—one of those rides that spins around and around and around, in an endless circle.

George used to go on something like it with his older brother Gunther whenever they went to an amusement park. Gunther always took the inside seat, and when the ride would start spinning, George always got smushed.

"Oh thank goodness!" a pimply teenager called out. "Now you can get me off here!"

"No, me! Get *me* off!" a sallow-faced woman cried. "It's my turn!"

"But I was only supposed to be on here for an hour!" a bony girl shouted.

"I have to go to the bathroom!" said a stringy man with an unkempt beard.

"SILENCE!" the dean shouted, and they all clammed up.

"What's that ride doing here?" George asked as Dean Dean Deanbugle finally put him down.

"That's the whirlyblerg."

George almost laughed. The whirlyblerg was an *amusement park* ride? He'd thought it was going to be some sort of horrible torture chamber.

"I can see the fear in your eyes. Good, good," Dean Dean Deanbugle said.

George tried to hide his sigh of relief by pretending he was quaking in his boots.

"Go on—I want you to ride with Lionel." The dean

dragged him across the room and strapped George into a car with the man who had shouted that he had to go to the bathroom.

The restraining belt clicked into place.

A girl in the car ahead of him turned around. "Please!" she said, her eyes wild beneath her tangled hair. "Please don't let him pull the lever! NOT THE LEVER!"

"What lev—" George said, but then was jerked forward as the whirlyblerg began to move. George looked to his right and saw the dean, waving good-bye next to a lever that came up from the ground. But then George's car whipped around the corner, and when it came back around, the dean was gone.

Around and around and around. George slid on top of Lionel, and Lionel smushed him back, and the two of them were like tumbled laundry, like scrambled eggs, like whipped cake batter, like tussling puppies.

"Sorry in advance, kid, but I get motion sickness. But they don't call it the whirly—*BLERGGGGG*!" Lionel leaned over the side of the ride and threw up. After a few more spins around the room, he wiped his mouth and said, "Like I was saying, they don't call it the whirlyblerg for nothing."

George winced and looked away as Lionel retched again.

"Can't Dean Dean Deanbugle give you a barf bag?" George said.

"You think he'd get me a barf bag?"

"Maybe," George said. "If you asked." A draft of wind slapped him in the face, and it seemed like the ride was starting to go—if possible—even *faster*. "How long have you been on this thing, anyway?"

"I have no idea!" Lionel said. "Sometimes Dean Dean Deanbugle will come down here and throw water bottles and food at us. Whatever we can catch is ours to eat."

George's head was spinning. Partially from the information, but mostly from the ride. "He *throws* food at you?"

Lionel nodded.

"If he's in a good mood, he'll throw solid food, like bread and cheese and pasta. If he's in a rotten mood, he'll throw us mushy food, like mashed potatoes, porridge, pudding, soup—things that are nearly impossible to catch."

George felt like he was going to be sick. He covered his mouth with his hands.

"I know that look," Lionel said as the ride jerked again. "If your last meal is coming back up, just let it."

George gripped the side of the car for a second—or a minute—or an hour—or a day—he wasn't quite sure. Finally he said, "I think I'm okay now."

"What did you do, kid?" Lionel said.

"I didn't perform well enough on a class assignment," George said. "What about you?"

"I went through a teenage rebellion phase, where I didn't want to listen to authority. But hey, I'd listen to authority now, I swear!"

A cry came from somewhere across the ride.

"And Hannah in front of you stole a plate of Dean Dean Deanbugle's pasta."

"Not worth it!" she groaned.

George was so dizzy he couldn't even see straight anymore. The rainbow walls swirled together. The happy music sounded like blended mush. And the ride kept going, faster and faster and *faster.*

"Why isn't the ride stopping?"

Hannah whipped around, her hair flailing. "It's broken, of course!"

"Broken! Broken how?"

"It never stops on its own. Someone needs to pull the lever, or it will keep going forever."

"And no one's ever escaped?"

"How could you?" she said. "Even if you *could* get the restraining belt off, you'd be flattened by the spinning cars! The only way to stop it is with the lever, but you'll never reach it from here. It's all the way across the room."

189

George was beginning to feel nauseous again. The ride flipped him like a burger, flopped him like pancake, and tossed him like a salad. Even with his eyes shut, George could feel his brain spin around and around and around like a pizza crust on a chef's finger.

He tried to distract himself by thinking of something else, but his thoughts came up as a jumble of incomprehensible words. How could he get off the whirlyblerg? Surely *someone* had escaped it. Who had he ever known that was on this thing?

"Reuben!" George blurted aloud. "Reuben Odell— was he ever here?"

"How do *you* know Reuben?"

"Is he here? Or did he escape?" George asked. If Reuben escaped, maybe it was possible to get off the whirlyblerg. Maybe it was possible to make it out of the school alive without graduating! "Please tell me he escaped!"

"Reuben *was* here for a while, but then Dean Dean Deanbugle plucked him off the ride. We don't know what happened to him after that."

No no no no no! A dead end! George suddenly felt like crying, but he was so dehydrated that he didn't have any tears inside him.

All the while, the whirlyblerg spun and spun and spun and spun and spun.

"We can't just sit here!" George said. "We have to escape . . . or at least try."

"BLERGGGGGGGG!" retched Lionel.

"Escape is impossible," Hannah said.

George dug into his pockets. There was nothing there, but he *was* wearing a belt. *Can I do anything with a belt?* he wondered. Lasso? Whip? Rope? Could any of these things stop the lever? Pickapocket's voice popped into his head: *Anything can be a gadget!*

George wiggled out of his belt. Since he was on the outside, he was closest to the lever. Whenever they spun near, George leaned to the side and tried to whip his belt far enough to reach the lever.

"Are you *insane*, boy? Aren't we all in enough trouble?" Lionel shouted when he realized what George was doing.

"Lionel, we can't just sit here and wait for the dean to come back. It might be forever!"

Lionel shook his head, and George went back to trying to hit the lever. But after what felt like hundreds of tries, he realized he was just too far away to reach. After a while, he wasn't sure how long he'd been there. It could have been hours or days or weeks.

At last, the door opened, and George saw a blurry figure come into the room. But he wasn't walking to the lever. George whipped around behind the center of the ride, and when he could see that side of the room again, the figure was throwing food.

"CATCH!" Lionel shouted, as packages of turkey jerky, loaves of bread, fistfuls of uncooked pasta, containers of cottage cheese, bushels of bananas, cartons of strawberries, bars of candy, jugs of lemonade, and bottles of water came soaring.

George caught three bananas, a chocolate bar, and a jug of lemonade.

He was so thirsty. He opened the lemonade straight away and drank greedily from it, but the ride was too bumpy, and he ended up getting a lot of it on his face.

George bent forward and stashed the food in the netting underneath the seat. To his surprise, Lionel seemed to already have a secret stash of food and drinks down there.

When he reemerged, George was shocked to see the blurry figure still standing there. Was he—yes! The figure was starting to walk over to the lever. Suddenly, the ride slowed, but when it finally stopped, George was certain his head did a few more loops around the track before it caught up with the rest of him.

The dean walked over to his car, and all of the prisoners fought against their restraints.

"George," Dean Dean Deanbugle said, lifting his seat belt. He pulled George off, pushed the dizzy Lionel back down, and locked the metal bar again.

"Please," George croaked. "Let the others off the ride!"

Dean Dean Deanbugle ignored him. "I think that's enough for now. I expect to see you at class on Monday, and you *will* have talent again."

George slumped. "Yes, sir."

"And George? If I ever see you slacking again, I'll make sure you stay on the whirlyblerg forever."

The Opposite of Thieving

After Dean Dean Deanbugle let him off the whirlyblerg, George trudged back to his room and sulked there the rest of the weekend. On Monday morning, he barely had the energy to get out of bed, but he knew that one more mess up would land him back on that horrifying whirly-blerg. So he made himself go to Ballyrag's class.

He collapsed into his usual seat and laid his head in his arms, waiting for class to begin.

"What happened to you over the weekend? Are you okay?" Tabitha asked. "I—I was so scared for you."

"I'm fine," George said firmly, keeping his head down. He definitely did *not* want to talk to her.

Moments later, Ballyrag entered the classroom, wearing two shoes around his neck. As he stood in front of the class, his mustache gave a twitch. It looked like a tiny rodent living on his face. "Now! Sit down, sit down. We're going to learn something specially important today."

George pulled out a pencil.

"Right now, we're going to be learning about basic grieving theory. So . . . let's start with kidnapping. What's the number one thing you have to remember about that? You gotta remember to hold them for handsome. So when you're holding someone for handsome, you need to send them a list of reprimands, and you got to make sure your note sounds very minister—yes, Miss Crawford?"

The whole class turned to look at Tabitha, whose hand was high in the air. "I think you're confused. We've already learned about ransom notes."

"We're learning it again. Now . . . what was I saying?" Ballyrag scratched his mustache. "Ah, yes, you have to hold someone for handsome. So when you're holding someone for handsome, you have to—yes?"

Tabitha raised her hand again. "But we've already learned this. And we haven't had any new students since the last time you taught it. So *no one* is learning anything new from this lesson."

Ballyrag coughed. "Uh . . . so you have to hold someone for handsome. And to do that, you must leave a handsome note. One that sounds very bad and minister—"

"Teach me something *new*," Tabitha said, standing up. She wasn't even raising her hand anymore.

George looked at her in awe and horror. Didn't she know what would happen if she didn't sit back down? She could end up on the whirlyblerg!

"Sit down, Tabitha," George whispered.

"I will *not* sit down!" she shrilled. Then she pointed a finger at Ballyrag. "Teach me something new!"

Ballyrag's eyes frantically darted around the room, and his mustache twitched. He clearly did not know what to do. "I . . . uh . . . a threat, a bequest, and constructions are the things you need to remember to make a good handsome note—"

"NO!" Tabitha shouted. "No! This is the *third* repeat lesson I've had to sit through. The first time I thought you were confused, and the second time I ignored it, but I'm *not* going to sit here and have you waste my time!"

George's jaw dropped. What was she *thinking?* How could she talk to a teacher like that?

"Now *teach me something new!*" she demanded. "I want to be challenged!"

Ballyrag blinked. "So . . . the first rule for making handsome notes—"

Tabitha slammed her books on the desk; Ballyrag jumped and began to whimper.

"NO!" she said again, so angry she was shaking. Her nostrils flared the way they always did when she was livid. "NO, NO, NO! STOP IGNORING ME!"

Ballyrag mumbled incoherent sounds into his mustache.

"FINE," Tabitha shouted, gathering her books in her arms and marching straight out of the classroom.

George gasped. The whole class began to murmur and chirp and gossip, while Ballyrag stood limply at the front of the classroom, like he had no idea what had just happened or what to do about it. "This has never happened before—somebody call Bean Bean Beandugle."

When the whole class kept whispering, Ballyrag grunted. "I told the Bean," he grumbled, "this is *exactly* why I need an asgarapus in my class—for emergences like this. *Now* how do I reach him?"

Asgarapus? George thought. He looked around to see if anyone else had heard Ballyrag, but it seemed like everyone was too busy chattering to pay him any attention. *Did Ballyrag mean asparagus? And how would a vegetable help him contact the dean?*

Eventually, Ballyrag's brain seemed to start working again, and he stiffened. "Nettle down! Nettle down!" he yelled, and he continued teaching about ransom notes.

But George couldn't concentrate on the lesson—his brain was stuck on Tabitha. He couldn't believe she just *walked out* of class like that. Where in the world did that come from? And what was she thinking? It was like she was *trying* to get herself thrown on the whirlyblerg!

He spent all afternoon and evening thinking about what she did. But after dinner, he couldn't afford to think about Tabitha anymore; he knew he needed to complete his homework—so that the dean had no excuse to put him back on the whirlyblerg ever again.

George crumpled into a chair near a poisonous prickled plant in the greenhouse and pulled out his assignment from Ballyrag.

Out of the corner of his eye, a potted shrub scuffled across the grass toward him.

"Hello?" George said to the rubber tree plant. "Who's there? Inside that plant?"

It seemed to waddle with a little more oomph when George called out to it, so he cooed, "Here . . . planty! C'mere, boy!"

The plant's body lifted, and George saw two brown ankles and a pair of sneakers shuffle toward him.

"I'm a *girl*," said Tabitha's muffled voice from inside

the base of the plant jar. Then she lifted the plant and crawled out the bottom.

"What are you doing in there?" George said.

"Hiding. I didn't want to get in trouble for skipping class all day."

"I can't believe you skipped class."

"*I* can't believe that's the third repeat lesson they're trying to make me sit through!"

She sighed and plopped down on the cobblestone walkway.

"What's wrong?"

"Aren't you still mad at me?" Tabitha said sadly.

George shrugged. "I guess. But you seem upset."

She looked around the room, and went around peering in bushes and peeking under rubber tree plants, just to make sure they were alone. Once she had inspected the place rather thoroughly, she came back to where George was sitting and wrung her hands together. "Okay . . . I just . . . I just wanted to say . . ." She looked down and winced. "I suppose. I guess. Maybe. I should just. Ugh."

"Are you okay?"

"IamreallyreallyreallyreallyreallyREALLYsorry," she said quickly. She winced like it caused her great pain to say it.

George raised his eyebrows.

"Look, George. Your friendship is more important to me than anything. I . . . I just wanted to let you know that I wasn't *really* mad at you. I just didn't want you to go away." She sighed. "I swear I didn't say anything to Dean Dean Deanbugle. And I don't know who did, but it wasn't me, I promise! I'd never want you to disappear or end up in the whirlyblerg—"

"Tabitha, I *was* in the whirlyblerg."

"You were . . . you were *what?*"

"That's where I was on Friday. Dean Dean Deanbugle took me to the whirlyblerg."

"What—how—are you—"

"It's a broken spinny amusement park ride, and I was on it for a day." He told her everything—about the room, about Lionel and Hannah, about the food and drinks that were thrown at the prisoners. Though, he was sure that he didn't quite capture the horror of being stuck on a circling ride that never ends. When he was done speaking, he buried his face in his hands.

"Don't do that," Tabitha said. "You can't get defeated, George! You just need an action plan. So . . . what are you going to do now?"

George looked around to make sure that no one was nearby, but it was just a bunch of wildflowers and small shrubs. Still, he lowered his voice. "I don't know.

I don't know what I *can* do. I guess I could graduate."

Tabitha nodded, eyes wide.

"But I don't know if I could. Or really, if I *would*." George sighed. "I just think I'd hate it . . . acting like I don't have a conscience. Pretending not to care about all those people I'd be stealing from. I don't think I'll be able to keep up my fake love of thieving for much longer . . . and then it's back to the whirlyblerg."

"You can get expelled," Tabitha whispered, looking around suspiciously, as if she was worried that the flowers had ears.

"I don't know how possible that is."

"You could do something good," Tabitha suggested.

"Good? Like what?"

"Well, thieves steal things, right? So what's the opposite of thieving?"

George blinked.

"*Giving back*, of course!" she said. "If you returned stolen items to their original owners, it'd be the total opposite of thieving."

"Yeah," George scoffed, "that sounds like the perfect way to be put on the whirlyblerg forever. Or be part of the waitstaff."

"Good point," Tabitha said, pulling a pencil out from behind her ear and rolling it between her fingers. She hummed thoughtfully. "It's like getting expelled doesn't exist here."

George scowled and slumped down even farther. Returning all the items in the mansion would definitely be a good way to counteract all of the thieving in Pilfer. But it was a ridiculously impossible idea. There were thousands—if not millions—of stolen items in Pilfer Academy; how could he possibly return them all? He was just one kid, and he'd surely be caught before he could complete the mission.

He was right back at the whirlyblerg again.

Okay, George thought as he watched Tabitha pensively chew on a pencil eraser, *maybe I could just return only the most important items*. But in a school full of stuff, who knew what the most important items were? It seemed like the whole stinking mansion was important.

George gasped.

"Tabitha!" he said so loudly that Tabitha threw up her pencil in fright. He dropped his voice again. "The whole mansion! The mansion is the key to everything!"

"What are you talking about, George?"

"I have to return the mansion! If I return the mansion, it would shut down the school forever."

Tabitha jumped to her feet. "George, that's *genius!*"

"Now all I have to do—"

"I?" she said, putting a hand on her hip. "I, I, I. Me, me, me. I don't hear any *we* here. What about me?"

"What about you?"

"I'm doing this with you," she said.

"What? But you *love* Pilfer!"

Tabitha sighed. "To tell you the truth . . . I don't. Ever since the midterm—"

"The midterm! You too?"

"But for a different reason than you," Tabitha explained. "At first, it just started with repeat lessons. I thought it was a mistake at first, but it wasn't. And then there are the teachers—they can't even speak correctly and make no sense. School's just not fun anymore because it's not a challenge. Every lesson, test, and homework assignment is just too easy, and I don't feel like I'm learning anything useful anymore."

"So . . . that's it? You want to leave Pilfer?"

"Don't get me wrong—I've had a great time here! But if I'm being asked to do the same tasks over and over again for months—or *years*—until our teachers randomly decide I'm ready to advance to year two, well then, it's just not worth all that wasted time. I want school to be challenging. I want to learn something new every day."

"Wow," George said. "Well . . . where will you go?"

"I don't know yet," she said thoughtfully. "I'll just

have to find a different school. Maybe one that isn't so illogical. There are plenty of great schools out there, and I want to go to the *best*." She hesitated. "For a while," she finally said, "I thought it was Pilfer. Because they make you feel really special. But it's all just part of their scheme. They make you feel important so that you don't realize that most of what they're teaching is absolute gibberish."

It was funny—he hadn't ever considered that Tabitha might want to leave Pilfer for her own reasons. But the more she opened up, the more he understood her thinking.

Tabitha looked at him fiercely. "The point is, George, that I'm all in. Let's return this mansion. You and me. Together."

"Tabitha, are you *sure* you want to do this with me? I mean, if we get caught, we'd be beyond toast. We're talking permanent waitstaff. Whirlyblerg for years. Or . . . worse."

"You need me," she said firmly. "And I need you, too. You're the best friend I've ever had, George. We're accomplices! Partners in crime!" She scrunched her nose. "Well, I guess now, partners in good deeds—"

George rushed forward and hugged her with a grip as strong as an alligator's chomp.

He was so glad they were friends again. Together they left the greenhouse and headed out into the very gray day. The sky was flat and dull, like construction paper.

They raced straight into the hedge maze since nothing was quieter or more private than being stuck between fifteen-foot hedges.

"But how do we return the mansion?" George asked as they got to the heart of the maze.

"Easy! With one perfectly placed phone call."

"A phone call? But . . . we have no phone! And even if we did, we couldn't call the police. We'd end up on the whirlyblerg."

"I know that!" Tabitha said. "We wouldn't be calling the police. We'd be calling France."

"France! What's in France?"

"Croissants," she said, and George looked at her incredulously. "I'm *kidding*, George. The Duke of Valois is in France!"

"And . . . ?"

"Honestly, George! The Duke of Valois has been chasing Dean Dean Deanbugle for thirty years. So all we have to do is tell him where to find us."

"But where is that, exactly?"

"Haven't the foggiest," Tabitha said, wrapping her

sweater even tighter around her. "But if we give the duke a vague area, then he can scout it out himself."

"And where are we going to find a phone? We can't call—"

George cut off.

Call. The word sparked his memory. *Somebody call the Bean Bean Beandugle,* Ballyrag had said that very morning. *This is exactly why I need an asgarapus in my class.*

"Asparagus!" George whispered, practically shaking with excitement. "Ballyrag said today—after you left—how he wished he had an asparagus, so he could call the dean from his classroom. Didn't he mention asparagus during your detention after our kitchen raid?"

Tabitha's jaw dropped. "Oh! Ballyrag told Strongarm that someone was on the asparagus—"

"And that time Dean Dean Deanbugle came and took over our class!" George interrupted. "He said Strongarm could use the asparagus instead of teaching—"

"It's a code word!" Tabitha squealed. "Asparagus is a code word for . . . for telephone!"

"And that door on the first floor—the one with the sign about asparagus—"

"There *has* to be a phone in there!"

George leaned against the hedge maze and found it to

be surprisingly prickly. "Why do you think they keep a phone in there? What's in that room?"

Tabitha gasped. "I bet it's the teachers' lounge!"

"Teachers' lounge? What makes you say that?"

"Every school has one! Teachers always have a secret, special place where they can go to gossip about students. And it would make sense to keep a phone in there."

Footsteps grew louder. A group of second-years ran past them, headed deeper into the heart of the maze.

"It has to be during Mischief Night," George said, lowering his voice. "With Mischief Night, curfew is off. If everyone's sneaking around the mansion playing pranks on everyone else, no one is going to notice us missing."

He started to feel a little wobbly, thinking about what they would do. By the end of the week, he'd either be forever free or forever whirlyblerged.

Tabitha gulped, looking slightly green herself. "So, we have a half-baked idea," she said sensibly. "And, what, you're thinking that our smarts and thieving talents will pull us through?"

"That," George said, "and a whole lot of luck."

Mischief Night

October 30th started out with a BANG.

Because a bunch of fourth-years set off fireworks on the roof.

From the first crack of sunrise, it seemed like everyone was getting ready for the night. People were stealing supplies, conferring in corners, and shouting threats. George and Tabitha were getting ready, too, but they weren't pulling off a prank. This was the real deal.

They ran through their plan about fifteen times, mostly on Tabitha's request. She wanted to nail down every detail exactly right: break into the teachers' lounge, find the phone, dial an operator, have her connect them to the Duke of Valois, and stay on the line with him until he could get the police to his house to trace the call to their location.

The problem—as George pointed out multiple times—was that they had no idea what to expect once they entered the teachers' lounge.

"We'll just have to wing it, George," she said, in a most un-Tabitha-like manner. "It's the best plan we've got."

By dinnertime, George was a nervous wreck. He pushed food around his plate but couldn't eat much of anything at all, even though Tabitha nagged him about sneaking around on an empty stomach.

"You need your energy," she said.

"Tabitha, please! If I'm not hungry, I'm not hun—"

BANG. Milo thumped his fists on their table. "I'm going to *destroy* you guys tonight!" he snarled.

"We don't care," Tabitha snapped. "We have something better to do tonight."

George kicked her under the table.

"Like what?"

Milo looked at them suspiciously, but they ignored him until he finally walked away. Then, George scarfed down a few bites of food. Milo was the *least* of his worries tonight.

After that, it was time. George and Tabitha headed back to the dorm and separated to pack their bags. George buzzed around his room, grabbing things he thought he might need and shoving them in his backpack: a flashlight, two pairs of gloves, and a small throw pillow. Then he ran around grabbing any and every object he would probably never need: extra-strength dental floss, socks, a baseball cap, bubblegum, a dustpan, a candle, and a broken mop that he stole from the janitor's closet.

He rushed back downstairs and waited fifteen minutes before he heard footsteps coming down the stairs.

But it wasn't Tabitha.

"You headed out for Mischief Night, George?" Robin said.

"Yeah. Soon."

Beth winked. "Hope you and Tabitha have something good to compete with us! We have the *best* prank planned."

"See you in the morning," Neal said with a wave. "And here's hoping we'll all be school legends by then."

Oh, I'll be a legend all right, George thought, his stomach writhing like a bucket of worms.

After they left, there was silence in the dorm's entrance corridor again. George stood up and paced the hall— what was taking Tabitha so long? Did she change her mind? Did she get knocked out or something?

THUNK.

THUNK.

THUNKITY-THUNK-THUNK.

THUNK.

It sounded like a ginormous man-eating monster was thumping down the stairs, and George's heart pounded.

A moment later, a ginormous man-eating *suitcase* tumbled down the stairs and landed with a *THUD* at the bottom. Tabitha came running after it.

"What are you doing? We can't pack our stuff!" He lowered his voice. "It's far too obvious!"

"This isn't for home," Tabitha whispered back. "These are all the thieving tools I can think of that we might possibly need."

"For crying out loud," George said, "just take what you can carry in a backpack."

Tabitha zipped open her suitcase and started to pull out a few things. She was packing so fast that George could barely see the objects she deemed worth taking, but he did notice that she slipped a dinner knife, paper clips, and a few books into her bag.

"By this time tomorrow we'll either be on the whirly-blerg or free," George said, his stomach giving quite a jolt.

Tabitha squeezed his hand.

Far from being deserted, every hallway was crackling with energy. Groups of friends were skulking together, shiftily glancing at other people to see what *they* were doing. The first-years looked a little nervous, the second-years looked eager, and third-years looked menacing. Even all the fourth-years were back on campus for the celebration—and they looked positively evil.

Tabitha led the way, and as they weaved in and out, they caught glances of some pretty impressive pranks in the works. A group of second-years was attempting to glue all the furniture in Ballyrag's classroom to the ceiling. Robin, Neal, Beth, and Becca were trying to steal the hands off of every clock in the school. Another cluster of first-years was trying to transport a big roll of bubble wrap, while a gang of third-years tried to steal it from them.

The fourth-years had the advantage of being able to go off campus, so they brought back supplies that no one else had. George couldn't see all of it as he rushed by, but their prank had something to do with purple hair dye, a leaf blower, and one very hungry llama.

At last, they were in the Ma Barker Wing, the barren, empty hall on the right-hand side of the first floor—the same wing that housed the Robin Hood Room and, according to Tabitha, the detention dungeon that hosted a piranha pit.

As they ran past the Robin Hood Room, three third-years were trying to break in. Clearly they weren't at the top of their class.

"If we just steal the trampoline . . ." one said.

"But how do we get it out? I hear it's *big!*"

"Hey! Kids!" the third one shouted, pointing at George and Tabitha. "Either of you got a key to this room?"

"Nope!" Tabitha lied, and they both quickly ran around the corner.

They sprinted all the way down the bare-bones corridor, right to the dead end area, where there were no exhibits, nothing gold or glittery or remotely fancy-pants. Just a single, unassuming door with that crazy sign:

CLEANING SUPPLIES AND VEGETABLE STORAGE
(ESPECIALLY ASPARAGUS)

George had never seen a teachers' lounge before—not at Pilfer or at his old school—but he thought that it would've looked like how he imagined a girls' bathroom: red carpets, couches, marble floors, lacy drapes, and a gum dispenser.

"This is it? I would've thought the entrance to the teachers' lounge would be a bit more . . . I don't know, classy."

"That's the genius of it," Tabitha said. "If they hang up a teachers' lounge sign, everyone would try to break in. And if the sign suggests that whatever's behind this door is dangerous or forbidden, it's like practically inviting students to try to sneak in. So they have to mark the door with something so utterly boring that no one would ever bother."

"If you say so," George said, reaching forward and putting his hand on the door. "Here we go." He took a deep breath, picked the lock in a matter of moments, and opened the door.

A Midnight Swim

It was pitch-black inside, and it seemed like the darkness was seeping out into the hall, trying to devour whatever light it could find. George dug into his bag for his flashlight and flicked it on.

Tabitha kept watch as George hopped inside. He shone his flashlight all around, but he couldn't see anything but a cat-sized door with a combination lock on it.

"Coast is clear in here, Tabitha! Come on in!"

She slipped into the room and shut the door behind her. George flashed his light on the combination lock, and Tabitha walked over to it. "I got this," she said, crouching near the door. She put her ear to the combination lock and began to twirl the dial. "The first number is forty-two."

"Great," George said, shining his flashlight on the ceiling. Some fat, round objects were high up in the rafters.

So high—and so deep in the shadows—that he could barely make them out. *What are they?* he thought. *Globes? Dodgeballs? Water balloons?*

"George!" Tabitha hissed. "I need that light!"

"Sorry!"

"The second number is zero."

They were silent as the dial was *click click click*ing.

He flashed his light up at the ceiling again. The balloons were bobbing up and down on the rafters.

"Uh . . . Tabitha?" he said as the objects began to move faster. "What is up there?"

She stopped turning the lock and looked up. "Pillows?" she said, squinting. "I don't know, George—but we don't have time! I need the light!"

He shone the flashlight on the combination lock again.

"Third number is twenty-seven. Got it!" Tabitha shouted, and the door popped open with a creak.

Suddenly, there came the noise of one enormous, collective *CLUCK!!!!*

Then the objects came plummeting down from their perches. George ducked as they zoomed past his head—pecking and flapping and flailing and floundering and squawking. Tabitha ran to help him.

"STRONGARM'S CHICKENS!" George yelped as twenty or more of them surrounded him and Tabitha.

They had wicked gleams in their eyes and looked rather hungry.

"The door, George! We have to get through the door!"

But the chickens stood between them and the way forward.

"*CLUCK, CLUCK, CLACK, CWAK!*" the chickens called angrily.

They looked evil. Murderous.

"We just have to make a run for it," Tabitha said. "Charge right into the chickens. Through is the only way out." She gulped. "Okay . . . here I go!" And she ran for it.

George followed behind her, and as they ran, the chickens began to nibble at their pant legs and peck their shoes. "OUCH!" George shouted as one nipped his ankle, and he gave it a big punting kick.

"*CLUCKKKKKKKKKKKKK!*" it screeched as it flew across the room.

"Touchdown!" George said, and with one last side-step, he dropped to his hands and knees—and crawled through the tiny door.

Tabitha closed it behind him, and they both leaned against it, panting.

"That was terrifying!" she said.

"I know," George wheezed. "I can still hear clucking."

"George—that's because you let a few in!"

Four chickens waddled toward them, inching closer and closer. "Ugh! Go away!" Tabitha cried as one got a good peck at the back of her ankle.

George looked up. This room was softly glowing, and it smelled like a doctor's office. But it was entirely, wholly, and completely empty. A single door stood directly across from them.

"Too easy! It's a trap!" Tabitha said, picking up the biting chicken and tossing it away from her.

The chicken squawked as it flew through the air, and it landed in the middle of the room. Then the floor crumbled, like it was made of sand.

DOWN

DOWN

DOWN

The chicken fell. The floor kept collapsing, stopping only at the very tips of George's and Tabitha's toes, and they backed against the wall as much as they could to avoid falling in. The pit was a perfect cylinder, and inside were wiggling, wriggling, flopping, flailing stringy things thrashing around.

"It's moving," George said. "Tabitha, the pit is *moving!*"

"Is that . . . a worm pit?"

"No . . . it's a spaghetti pit!" George gasped as he watched the noodles churn in a giant stirring pot beneath them.

At that moment, three chickens ran off the ledge into the pit. They clucked with glee and began pecking the spaghetti.

"How are we going to get across?"

Tabitha looked around. "I don't know," she said faintly. "I think our best bet is to suction ourselves to the wall and crawl. Did you bring plungers?"

"What are you two doing?" said a familiar voice from right behind them. They whipped around—Milo.

"No," said Tabitha. "No, no, no, no, no, no, no."

George gave Milo a hefty glower. "Are you following us?"

"Is this your Mischief Night prank?"

"None of your business," George said coolly.

"Go away, Milo," Tabitha said.

Milo rubbed his buzz-cut head like it was a genie lamp that was about to give him three wishes. "You're doing something bad, aren't you?"

"Yes, it's our horrible rotten prank—now leave us *alone*."

"Why are you here?" George said. "To, er, ruin our prank?"

"You're trying to escape from Pilfer, aren't you?"

"W-what?" George stammered. "What are you talking about?"

"Don't play dumb with me. I've spied on you a lot—"

"We know," George and Tabitha said together.

Milo scowled. "Let me say, it's been extremely *boring*

219

most of the time. But I finally overheard something useful when you said you didn't want to be at Pilfer anymore. When I went to Dean Dean Deanbugle, I was sure he'd throw you out or lock you up—"

"You *what*?" Tabitha shrieked.

George looked down at his shoes. He couldn't even believe he'd ever accused Tabitha of betraying him. Suddenly he felt like a fool.

But Tabitha skipped straight to anger. "You complete *numbskull*!" Tabitha shouted, putting her hands around Milo's neck and actually throttling him. "Did you *want* George to go to the whirlyblerg?"

"Whirl! Blerg!" Milo choked.

"Tabitha! Let go!"

Milo's face was turning almost purple, and he pushed Tabitha to get her off him. They both grappled and wrestled and tussled, tumbling forward—

"NOOOOOOOOO!" George shrieked as the two of them fell into the spaghetti pit and disappeared beneath the noodles.

At last, Tabitha's hand popped out of the top of the noodle pit, and she wiggled herself up. She took one gasping breath before Milo swam her way, and they began to wrestle in the noodles again.

"AUGH!" Milo said, pulling her hair.

"ERGH!" Tabitha replied, pushing him off her.

George ran his hands through his hair. It was up to him to get everyone out of the whirring, churning pasta pit—before Tabitha and Milo killed each other.

He reached into his backpack and tried to find anything useful, and his hands closed around the dental floss. *Everything is a gadget.* George unwound the whole string and lowered it into the pit—but it wasn't nearly long enough. He was about three inches short of reaching Tabitha's outstretched arms.

"Come on!" she shouted. "Send more down!"

"That's all I have!"

"Wait!" Tabitha said, inching herself as far up as she could, though it seemed difficult to stand on shifting spaghetti. When she finally got her footing, she could *just* reach the floss.

"You can do it!" George shouted down at her.

"George?" said Tabitha.

"Yeah?"

"Stop talking! I need to concentrate!"

Tabitha's fingertips brushed the floss, but she was too short to grab it. She pawed at the floss like a cat swipes at dangling string.

"Milo," she said. "Make yourself useful and lift me up a bit."

"You're going to leave me in the pit if I help you reach that string!" Milo protested.

"Will not! You can grab onto my foot."

"Let me go first!"

"No way! You'll leave *me* behind, and I can't reach!"

They continued to bicker, and George let out a shaky breath. This fight could go on forever, and they really needed to move forward before they were caught by a teacher trying to get into the lounge.

"Tabitha," George called down the pit, "we're wasting time. Let Milo go first. Then we can both help you up. Promise, Milo?"

"Fine. Promise," he said grumpily, and he treaded through the spaghetti to the dangling floss. He was a few inches taller than Tabitha, which put him at a perfect height to grab the string.

"Pull me up, George!"

George tugged on the extra-strength floss with all his might. The string dug painfully into his hands, but he kept on pulling. It was like a tug-of-war that he had to win.

At last, Milo's hand reached the platform, and George ran to the edge to pull him up out of the pit. With a yank, tug, *pull*, George dragged Milo onto the ledge, and they paused there for a moment.

"Okay," George said, helping Milo to his feet. "Do you

have any gadgets for Mischief Night that we can use? Like more string to tie to our denta—*AHHHHHHHHHHHH!!!!*"

Without warning, Milo pushed George into the pit. He squashed right into the spaghetti.

"SUCKERS!" Milo shouted, and there came a sound like a door slamming shut.

Tabitha gritted her teeth. "That no good, backstabbing, little—"

"He's going to tattle on us!" George said in horror. "I bet he's going to get Dean Dean Deanbugle right now!"

"I hope the rest of those chickens peck his eyes out," Tabitha grumbled.

"We have to hurry. How do we get out of here? I have nothing useful in my backpack."

The pit churned, and they swirled around with the spaghetti. All the stirring reminded him of a slower whirlyblerg, and the thought made him nauseous.

"My backpack! That's *it!*" Tabitha said. "I lost my backpack during the fall into the pit, but I have extremely adhesive tape inside! If we can find my bag in the spaghetti, we can get the sticky tape and use it to climb up and across the wall."

A wave of spaghetti came tumbling toward him, and George strained to keep his head above the noodles. "I'll dive down and try to find your bag!"

"Be careful!" Tabitha shouted.

George gulped an enormous breath and sank beneath the spaghetti. He did the breaststroke through noodles and reached around blindly for Tabitha's backpack. Every time he took a breath, he seemed to get noodles up his nose.

His hand brushed something—

"*Cluck!*"

Rats! he thought. *Just a chicken that sunk to the bottom.*

He fumbled around, hands outstretched, certain that he was tying himself into some huge spaghetti knot. He ate a few strands of pasta, but they tasted a little mushy and overcooked. In the distance, he thought he heard Tabitha shouting, but it sounded muffled. He moved his right hand forward. Nothing. He moved his left hand forward. Nothing. He moved his right foot—*whump!*

His foot hit something small and lumpy—Tabitha's backpack.

He did a front flip in the noodles, grabbed the bag, and propelled himself upward.

"Found it!" he said as he broke the surface.

"Took long enough!"

George kicked his feet, treading pasta. He already felt himself slipping down again, being dragged under by spaghetti arms. "I had to eat my way out! That takes time!"

"So much time," Tabitha said, "that I was beginning to think the noodles had eaten *you*!"

They dug the tape out of Tabitha's bag. Then Tabitha wrapped the tape around George's hands—sticky side out—before doing her own. They swam over to the wall, put their hands against it, and began to crawl up.

The sticky tape gave George a few slippery scares, but it held his weight all the way up. Tabitha followed, as fast and nimble as a centipede.

Standing in front of a new door, they brushed themselves off and walked in quickly. They'd lost so much time swimming in spaghetti; they had no more to waste.

But as soon as Tabitha closed the door behind them, the lights flicked off, and red laser beams zoomed across the room. They zigzagged and crossed in every-which-direction, humming with the sound of impending doom.

"Through is the only way out," Tabitha said meekly, and George gulped.

Zzzzzzzzzzzt!!!

"This is just *great*," Tabitha said, tossing her hands up. "We don't learn how to dodge lasers until third year!"

George fished a sock out of his bag and threw it into the middle of the room. *ZZzzzzzzzt!!!!* It hit a laser and exploded into a cloud of dust.

"Yup," he said. "They're deadly."

"What do we do?" Tabitha whispered. "We can't cross this! We'll be toasted alive!"

George frowned. As far as he could see, they had two options: turn back or move forward. He knew what was waiting for him if he turned back. It might be the safer choice—but it was one he didn't want to make. He *needed* to get out of Pilfer. And if he didn't go forward now, he wasn't sure when he'd have an opportunity like this again.

"I have to keep going," George said. "I have to try."

Tabitha side-eyed the lasers nervously. "I want to try, too. I just hope we don't regret it later."

"We'll be really careful. Now, who first?" George said, and they both shouted, "NOT IT!" at the same time.

But someone had to be first. George swallowed his fear with one ginormous gulp. "Okay, fine. I'll go." He stepped forward, so nervous he was almost feverish.

"You can do it, George!" Tabitha said, and that boosted his confidence a bit. "Concentrate!"

George gingerly slipped himself between two lasers. Then stooped under three more. Then tiptoed over one. It was a slow process, and he had to make sure he was as attentive as possible. There was no room for mistakes, or he would be fried to a crisp. He ducked, crawled, slithered, jumped, inched, twisted, and maneuvered through the laser beams. Very slowly. Carefully.

Zzzzzzzzzt!!!

"GEORGE! LOOK OUT!"

He looked down at his pants. There was a big hole in the fabric around his knee, but the laser missed his leg by a centimeter.

"Pay attention!" Tabitha called.

A droplet of sweat slid down the back of his neck.

"Tabitha," he said hoarsely, "you should start making your way through. We don't have time!"

"Okay," she said. He could tell that she was scared, but she was hiding it well.

George continued to slink, wiggle, and weave his way through, taking every step very sluggishly and cautiously. Arm under this one, leg over that one, head between these two, body going sideways. *One at a time,* he reminded himself often. *Just take one at a—*

ZZzzzzzzzt!!! came the sound from across the room.

"What's that?" George shouted. He was stuck between three lasers and couldn't see her. "Tabitha! Did you get hit?"

Silence.

"Tabitha!"

Silence.

"TABITHA! ARE YOU OKAY?"

There came a slight sobbing sound.

His heart was lead. "Are you hurt?"

"It—it—it's my braids!" she said mournfully. "That stupid laser just cut off half my hair!"

Relief and rage surged through him. "DON'T SCARE ME LIKE THAT!"

"Sorry!" she said. "I was just stunned!"

He hopped over a low laser. "Good thing it wasn't your head! Be careful out there!"

"I'm trying!"

He continued on. Over, under, sideways, up, down, around. It seemed to take forever—like he'd *never* get untangled from these hot, buzzing lasers.

But at last, George reached the end. He was perfectly fine, but his pants had suffered; they were so holey that they looked like Swiss cheese.

He brushed himself off. It had been impossible to see this side of the room when he was so busy focusing on not getting burned up by lasers, but now that he was here, he took a look around. On this side of the room, there was no door—just a single tube slide that led to who-knows-where.

He turned back to look at Tabitha. She was about three-quarters of the way through the lasers, taking it a little faster than he had, but proving—like always—that she was talented at anything she put her mind to.

After what felt like forever, Tabitha crawled out from underneath the last laser, and George helped her to her feet.

She held a hand over her heart, and her face was glistening with sweat. George thought the accidental haircut made her look a bit tough.

He led her to the tube slide.

"I bet this is it!" George said.

"How can we know this leads to the teachers' lounge?"

Tabitha said skeptically. "Maybe this leads to a trap."

"I don't see any other choice," George said. "If we want to escape Pilfer, we *have* to keep moving forward. And this is the only way. Unless you want to go *back* through the lasers again."

Tabitha shook her head.

"Then here we go!" And he jumped into the tube and slid. *"AHHHHHHHHHHH!"* he shouted as he twisted and turned through pitch blackness. Round and round and round and round, down and down and down and down—until he was spit out, right on top of a beanbag chair. Then, not a moment later, Tabitha tumbled on top of him, and the force of both of them split the beanbag. Thousands of beads rolled out all over the floor.

Immediately, George knew they had found the teachers' lounge, because it made the Robin Hood Room look like a dungeon. The walls were lined with soda machines, candy dispensers, and full buffets of deep-fried everything. The room glowed, golden and brilliant and warm, like an underground sun.

And there—on the table—was a beautiful, diamond-encrusted phone, just waiting for use. George walked over to it. His heart was pounding.

"Ready?"

Tabitha nodded.

George picked up the phone and put it to his ear—when someone fell down the slide and smacked to the floor with a groan.

"Oh! My back!" Dean Dean Deanbugle groaned as he stood up from the floor, slipping on some of the loose beans. "I was the *only one* who voted for an orzo-stuffed chair. But it would have been so much more comfortable."

A machine operator sung into George's ear. *Your call cannot be completed as dialed. Please hang up and try again.*

"Hang up," said Dean Dean Deanbugle, baring every single one of his terrible teeth. "If you don't want to be strapped in the whirlyblerg for the rest of your livelong days, you'll hang up this *moment*."

George hung up the phone.

1-800-We're-in-Trouble

There was no way around it: They were caught.

George glanced at Tabitha, who looked frightened to the point of tears. He knew that he had to come up with a plan—lightning fast.

"Who were you talking to?" Dean Dean Deanbugle said. "Did you just call the police?"

Tabitha squeaked. "We didn't call any—"

"Any of the police," George said. "We placed a call to the Duke of Valois. He's on his way here right now to pick up his mansion."

Tabitha's eyes bugged out, but Dean Dean Deanbugle didn't seem to notice. His face went ghostly white, and his hands shook wildly. "You called the Duke of Valois?"

"Of course," George said.

"Absolutely," Tabitha said.

"But *how*?"

"We placed a collect call. Operators connected us."

The dean ran to the phone, picked it up, and began frantically dialing in numbers. Beads of sweat formed on his forehead and trickled down his face.

George was holding his breath—the room was so silent he was sure he'd be able to hear an amoeba move.

Dean Dean Deanbugle was waiting, his ear pressed to the ringing receiver. George could hear it very clearly from where he stood. When the call finally patched through, the conversation ping-ponged back and forth so much that George could barely keep track.

The Duke: *Allô?*

The Dean: Hello!

The Duke: *Alors?*

The Dean: (extraordinarily long pause) It's me.

The Duke: (extraordinarily longer pause) You! You— you fiend! Eet's been seven years since you've called on zis number. And ten years since I last found you in ze Americas with your . . . your school of leetle criminals.

The Dean: I don't know what those kids told you—

The Duke: Kids? What kids?

The Dean: Oh, so *that's* how you want to play it!

The Duke: Play what?

The Dean: (growling) You think you're so shrewd! So

233

clever! Well, I *know* that Beckett and Crawford contacted you. I know you're on your way.

The Duke: *Excusez-moi?*

The Dean: DON'T PLAY MIND GAMES WITH ME! I KNOW THAT I KNOW HOW I KNOW WHAT I KNOW!

The Duke: All *I* know iz zat you 'ave my 'ouse. And I *weel* get it back.

The Dean: It's *my* house now! FINDERS KEEPERS, LOSERS WEEPERS!

The Duke: You deedn't *find* it! You *stole* it! And I deedn't lose it! I left for *'alf an 'our* to go to ze *café* with my *wife*!

The Dean: Well, you shouldn't have left it behind—

The Duke: I am ze victim 'ere! 'ow iz zis my fault?

George's brain was whirring. He looked at Tabitha, but she was clearly panicking. It was all up to him—all he had to do was to somehow get to that phone. If he could just tell the duke where they were. But he knew that the second he started screaming for the duke, Dean Dean Deanbugle would just hang up.

He had to get Dean Dean Deanbugle *himself* to say it.

"We told him the exact coordinates of our school, sir!" George said suddenly. "We charted stars for months and figured it out—"

Tabitha squeaked, "We used the primary sources from

the library! Galileo, Copernicus, and Tycho Brahe!"

George had no idea what Tabitha was saying, but he nodded and added, "I'm so sorry that we told the duke where to find us—I regret it now!"

Dean Dean Deanbugle pulled the receiver away from his mouth. "You told him we were at Latitude 43.05, Longitude 75.38? Are you crazy?"

George tried to hide his shock—he couldn't believe the dean fell for his trick. He feared his expression might give away everything, and he silently hoped that the dean wasn't looking at him too closely.

But the dean didn't seem to be paying any attention to George. Or Tabitha for that matter. He was clearly far too panicked. His sweat-soaked eyebrows clung to his clammy forehead; he looked like a hairless cat that took a miserable swim in a bathtub.

The dean began to pace. "Listen, Nicolas!" he shouted into the phone. "The information the kids gave you is wrong. We are south. *Very far south.* In fact, we're so south that I'm getting sunburn."

And without another word, the dean slammed the receiver on the phone. Then he ran over to the wall, smashed open a glass case, and pressed a big red button.

At once, an earsplitting, headache-throbbing, mind-numbing, nerve-aching alarm began to screech.

WARNING! WARNING! WARNING! it blared. *CODE RED! ACTIVATE EMERGENCY RELOCATION PLAN! WARNING! WARNING! WARNING!*

George and Tabitha had to cover their ears.

But not for long—Dean Dean Deanbugle grabbed George and Tabitha by the wrists and roughly dragged them across the room.

Tabitha found her courage first. "Where are you taking us? To the whirlyblerg?"

Dean Dean Deanbugle did not answer her, which terrified George even more. Instead, the dean simply knocked on a part of the wall, and out popped a drawer with a lever inside. Dean Dean Deanbugle flicked the switch, and the whole wall folded outward to reveal a long, rickety staircase leading down.

Dean Dean Deanbugle shoved George and Tabitha into a chamber so silent that it blocked out the sound of the blaring alarm entirely. As he pushed them down the steps, Tabitha and George exchanged a dark look. But there was no way to escape. Dean Dean Deanbugle was hulking behind them, and there was nowhere to go but down.

"How did you find us so quickly? Milo, right?" George asked.

"Mr. Hubervick *was* running out as I was running in,

but there was a silent alarm that alerted me first. We might let students rot in spaghetti pits for a while, or get singed by lasers to teach them a lesson about prying into asparagus closets, but *just in case*, we need to be notified if an intruder gets too far."

A silent alarm! Of course. Just like the time he raided the kitchen with Tabitha. He should have known.

There was a chill in the staircase, and Tabitha shivered. The stairs twisted like a piece of fusilli, and the more steps they took, the darker it became. George was certain they were heading right back to the basement. To the whirlyblerg. He couldn't—simply *couldn't*—live the rest of his life on a never-ending roller coaster.

George turned around—Dean Dean Deanbugle's eyebrows were furrowed so low on his face that it looked like he might accidentally eat them. "Why? *Why* did you do this?"

George was silent. He thought that the dean might not appreciate his musings on how he was choosing to be a better person going forward.

"Happy Mischief Night?" Tabitha squeaked.

"What you did is unspeakable!" Dean Dean Deanbugle cried. "This was beyond a Mischief Night prank. You have almost *destroyed* my life's work. Luckily, we'll be moving the school momentarily."

George's heart thudded. By the time the Duke of Valois arrived, the mansion would be long gone. After *all that*, Dean Dean Deanbugle was just going to transport Pilfer Academy across the country.

At last, they reached a door at the bottom of the staircase, which led into a hallway full of chaos. George tried to wriggle out of Dean Dean Deanbugle's grip and into the throng of panicking students, but the dean kept a firm grasp on his arm. The alarms were piercing, people were blindly running into one another, and a bunch of students were nicking small things from the exhibits and pocketing them—just in case.

But if George thought the students were frenzied, they were nothing compared to the teachers. Strongarm ran past, her bony arms flailing in the air like two wild kite strings. "SAVE THE ICE CREAM! SOMEBODY SAVE THE ICE CREAM! SAVE THE TRIPLE-DIPPLE ULTRA-DELUXE MELTY CREAMY CREAMER RAINBOW SWIZZLE MILK MUNCH!"

And the others—Browbeat, Ballyrag, Pickapocket, Bagsnatcher, Nurse Embezzle, and a few George didn't recognize—were bouncing around the grand hall, screaming wildly.

"There you are!" Browbeat shrieked, when he spotted Dean Dean Deanbugle. He ran up to them with the rest of the staff. "We've been looking for you everywhere!"

"What's going on?" Ballyrag said. "Are we really moving vocations?"

"These little noodle-brains told the duke where to find us!" Dean Dean Deanbugle shouted.

"Bravo!" said Strongarm. "How sneaky!"

"Well done, well done! An A+ for you!"

"Happy day for stealthery!"

"THIS IS NOT A GOOD THING, YOU GORMLESS FOOLS!" Dean Dean Deanbugle shouted, a vein on his forehead popping.

"Oh, yes, right! Very naughty, children! Very naughty, indeed!" the teachers scolded. Then they scratched their heads . . . except for Ballyrag, who stroked his glorious golden mustache.

"NOW, TELL ME—WHY HAVE YOU ALL BEEN PANICKING?" the dean roared. "WE HAVE AN EMERGENCY ACTION PLAN. WE HAVE PRACTICED THESE DRILLS TWICE A YEAR, EVERY YEAR, FOR THE PAST TEN YEARS."

"Oh, we forgot," Strongarm said as Neal ran straight into her and fell on his bottom. "What do we have to do again?"

George tried wrenching his arm away from Dean Dean Deanbugle again, but he couldn't get free.

"You aren't going *anywhere*, Beckett!" the dean howled. Then he turned to address the teachers. "I'm going to take these children down to the whirlyblerg for ETERNITY. I've already pressed the button, and the new coordinates were selected years ago, so any moment now—"

RUMBLEEEEEEEEE.

The ground shook.

GRUMBLEEEEEEEEE.

Vases began to crash.

BRUMBLEEEEEEEEE.

The floor splintered beneath them.

"EARTHQUAKE!" the teachers shouted.

"EARTHQUAKE!" the students echoed.

"IT'S NOT AN EARTHQUAKE!" the dean roared. "PILFER ACADEMY IS ON THE MOVE!"

The mansion shook; the walls quivered. Dean Dean Deanbugle yanked George and Tabitha to the windows. "Keep your eyes on that vent!" Dean Dean Deanbugle shouted as he pointed to one on Pilfer's outer wall.

With a loud *screech*, the vent opened like a mailbox flap, and six spidery metal legs crawled out of the hole. They stretched their way to the ground, and when they were perfectly curved, they pushed against the earth, and the mansion shook again.

George looked to the left and saw another vent opening up, revealing its gigantic legs. Each time a group of legs hit the ground, the mansion shuddered violently.

"Five vents open, one to go!" shouted the dean, clasping George's wrist so tightly that he stopped being able to feel his fingers.

George couldn't see the last vent from his window, but the school shook all the same. Then with a sound like a kiss, the mansion rose off the ground, just high enough to pull the basement out from underground.

Dean Dean Deanbugle smiled proudly. "Pickapocket's crowning jewel. She stole them from a research facility that was creating machinery inspired by dung beetles."

"Dung beetles?" Tabitha asked.

"Dung," George snickered.

"Dung beetles can lift more than a thousand times their own body weight. And so, too, can Pilfer Academy's legs."

The mansion shook again as the legs began to move. The mansion scampered across the hill, barreling into the gate. It scuttled down the road, toward town, but then it turned at the last second and started to scurry across some empty fields. It moved faster than George thought possible for a massive building.

"Okay, we are on our way," the dean sighed in relief. But then he turned to George and Tabitha, gripping their arms a little tighter. He stared at them as if they were the most hideous things he had ever seen—like they were tarantula burgers. Like they were blankets made of boogers. Like they were stinky, smelly, putrid piles of rancid fish. "And now," Dean Dean Deanbugle snarled, "it's time to deal with *you*."

A Most Indecent Temper Tantrum

George tried to twist around, but he couldn't get a good angle on the dean. Tabitha was wrestling with his other arm.

"YOU WILL NEVER SEE THE LIGHT OF DAY AGAIN!" Dean Dean Deanbugle howled, pulling them away from the window.

"Not if we can help it!" said a voice from across the hall.

George looked up. A crowd of waitstaff and janitors were standing on the grand staircase, their arms full of kitchen tools. George recognized the balding waiter, the one doing the shouting in front.

"What are you all doing?" the dean hissed. "Get back to work before I th—"

"Union strike!" shouted a young freckled woman in

front, banging a spoon on the pot she was holding. The staff cheered.

"YOU DON'T HAVE A UNION!"

"Well, then, this is just a NORMAL REVOLT!"

"NORMAL REVOLT!" shouted the crowd. And they charged, banging pots and pans, waving spatulas and mops, brandishing brooms and bottles of cleaning solution.

"GET THEM!" the dean shouted at his staff.

"B-but I teach Stealth!" Browbeat said. "I deal with sneaky, sly attacks. I don't know how to fight."

"Nor I!"

"Me too!"

"Mmmmm!"

"Apologies, sir!" Strongarm said, and she ran away from the charging staff.

But just as the waitstaff was close enough to whop the dean over the head with a mop, the mansion shook violently, and everyone toppled over. The dean accidentally let go of George's and Tabitha's wrists, and they both went tumbling into the wall.

The dean popped back up immediately and dove for them. George tried to grab Tabitha by the hand and run. But Tabitha pointed to the window and shouted, "LOOK!"

Outside, a legion of planes in V formation had hooked

enormous chains onto Pilfer Academy of Filching Arts and was flying upward. The mansion quaked again as it was plucked from the ground like a weed.

As Pilfer swung from side to side, exhibits toppled over—pictures and tapestries were tumbling off the walls, and a giant stone statue fell over and cracked right down the middle. There came sounds of glass shattering and students screaming. A wave of lemonade from the fountain in the foyer spilled over and drenched a bunch of third-years, who ran into the hall, shrieking. Wind whooshed through the open windows, creating an enormous draft.

George shivered. He could barely make it out in the darkness, but it seemed as though each of the planes dropped a French flag from the window. His heart leaped with a giddy sort of hope.

The dean gasped and hugged the windowpane.

"DEAN DEAN DEANBUGLE!" said a voice from the megaphone. "THE DUKE OF VALOIS WOULD LIKE TO BID YOU *BONJOUR*. AND VERY SOON, *ADIEU*!"

"NO NO NO! YOU'LL NEVER CATCH *ME*!" Dean Dean Deanbugle shouted, and he jumped out the window.

It was an impressively large drop. But the dean was like a cockroach you just couldn't crush.

For a moment, George scanned the dark ground for Dean Dean Deanbugle and couldn't see a thing. But then, suddenly, a helicopter swooped down, illuminating everything in its beam lights. Dean Dean Deanbugle lay sprawled where he had landed—right in the middle of a field. Taking a cue from the dean, it seemed like all of the students and teachers were now grabbing prized items and pieces of Pilfer's finest exhibits in their arms—and jumping out of the mansion, leaving a bread-crumb trail of thieves and precious stolen goods across the ground.

"Out of my way!" snarled Milo from behind George.

He and Tabitha turned around.

Milo looked *furious*. He was holding one of the presidential mattresses, though it seemed like he'd rather prop it against the wall and use it as a punching bag. "You've ruined everything!" Milo spat at George and Tabitha.

"No, we didn't!" George said. "We're *saving* everything. Not like you'd understand."

Tabitha folded her arms. "Get lost, Milo!"

"I'm going to keep on thieving! Forever!" Milo beat his fist on his chest. "PILFER FOREVER!"

"I can't wait until the day you get arrested," Tabitha said coolly.

Milo blanched. Then he hopped up onto the windowsill, unlatched the window, and jumped out, the mattress beneath him to cushion the fall.

George rushed to the window—it was too dark to see, but he heard Milo shouting.

"Good-bye, Milo!" George cheered, and Tabitha whooped.

The stream of jumping students and teachers had mostly stopped, except for one window, where a few kids were escaping using hang gliders. From afar, he recognized Robin's curly hair.

"Hey, wait a minute," George said to Tabitha. "Those are our friends! HEY, GUYS!" he called, but they were too far away to hear him.

His friends kept screaming things into the night that sounded an awful lot like, "HOME!" and "FREEDOM!" They each launched themselves off the ledge and glided into the darkness of the night.

He felt happy, watching them soar away. He remembered how, on the very first day he'd met them, Beth and Becca had said they missed their parents. George hoped that they—and *all* his friends—would be reunited with their families soon.

"George!" Tabitha said. "The dean!"

She pointed back to the field, where Dean Dean Deanbugle was writhing around on the ground. Then he

began to kick his legs and throw the biggest temper tan-
trum George had ever seen. His wails echoed into the
night sky. He beat his fists and pulled at his eyebrows. He
snozzed onto his sleeve. He punched the living stuffing
out of a scarecrow. He ran around like a rabid dog, curs-
ing the day that George and Tabitha had been born and
vowing for revenge.

"REVENGEEEEEEEEEEEEEEEE!" his voice echoed
up, until it was drowned out by the sound of plane
engines and the roaring wind.

The people who had jumped out grew smaller and
smaller, but just before their faces were indistinguish-
able, George saw, from a distance, flashes of red and blue
lights headed toward the area.

The police were coming for Dean Dean Deanbugle, and
it made George oddly happy to feel like justice was about
to be served.

Everything was right again with his world: The dean
would be carted off to prison; he and Tabitha wouldn't
be forced to steal; the mansion was returned to its right-
ful owner; and Pilfer Academy of Filching Arts was over.

Everything was perfectly peachy . . . except for one
thing.

They were ascending into the clouds on a one-way
ticket to France.

George and Tabitha leaned out the windows of the school and shouted to the pilot. "HELLO!" they shrieked. "HELLO! HELLO! PUT US DOWN! STOP THE MANSION! STOP! STOP! STOP!"

But no one could hear them over the roar of the engines and howling wind.

At last, they finally had to accept that they were being kidnapped *again*. They just hoped it would turn out better this time.

When George turned back around, the waitstaff were shedding their Pilfer patches and stomping on them furiously.

"Thank you," George said, turning to the balding waiter and the rest of the staff. "You guys saved us."

"It was the least we can do for you kids. It's been a long while since anyone cared about our well-being."

George held out a hand. "What's your name?" George said.

"Reuben," the balding ex-waiter said. "Reuben Odell."

George and Tabitha gasped.

"You were right here this whole time!" Tabitha exclaimed.

"What happened to you after the whirlyblerg?"

"Dean Dean Deanbugle made me part of the waitstaff," Reuben said. "For years, I was too afraid to fight back or escape—we all were. Dean Dean Deanbugle often threatened to put us back on the whirlyblerg forever to keep us in line."

"And speaking of the whirlyblerg," George said, "there are people still on it—Lionel and Hannah and everyone else."

"We'll take you there!" a woman said. And they all began to run toward the side door that led to the dungeons.

When they reached the hallway full of putrid, rotting pumpkins, George knew they were close. And when they reached the entrance, George didn't hesitate one second. He kicked the door open, ran to the lever, and shut down the ride. Then the waitstaff helped everyone off.

While most of the whirlyblerg victims stretched their limbs, Lionel ran straight for the bathroom. Afterward, they all gathered in the ballroom. Lionel, Hannah, and the other people on the whirlyblerg had a million zillion questions, and George and Tabitha explained what had happened.

"He was pure evil," a gangly-looking woman said when they finally finished speaking.

"The police have him now," George said.

"Good," Lionel replied. "He deserves that. And worse."

They sat around talking for a few hours, but then people began to doze off. Maybe it was the soothing *whoosh* of the wind outside, or maybe it was the way the mansion swung back and forth, like a giant cradle beneath the planes. But soon everyone was all curled up and snoring.

Except George. He was still too hyper. He turned to Tabitha, whose eyes were closed. He couldn't tell if she was sleeping or not. "Pssssst! Tabitha! Are you awake?"

"Of course," she said immediately, not opening her eyes. "How could I possibly sleep right now?"

George sat up. "Let's go then!"

Together, they tiptoed out of the ballroom and wandered around Pilfer, full of giddy excitement and dizzying relief.

"We did it!" George said. "I can't believe we pulled this off."

Tabitha nodded. "Of course we did—we're both top of our class."

"We *were* top of our class," he said. "But I'm sure you'll be top, no matter where you go next," he added.

They drifted into the room with enormous chandeliers and forty-foot mirrors with gold trim. They looked at their reflections, and what they saw was pretty awful. Between the two of them, they had torn-up clothes, scratches, scrapes, lopsided hair (in Tabitha's case), and a few blossoming bruises.

"Let's keep walking," Tabitha said. "After all, it's our very last night in this mansion. Ever."

In every room and every corridor, George was surprised to find how empty the school was. Most of the valuable items had been pushed out the windows already or nabbed by students and teachers. Only a few enormously heavy items remained. The fighter plane was still in the foyer. The T-rex was there, too, but it was missing a bunch of the bones on its legs.

They wandered upstairs, and after hours of circling the wings and recounting the night's events in every detail, they found themselves sprawling on the couches in the dorm's narrow entranceway.

George let out an earthshaking yawn. "Don't let me fall asleep!" he groaned.

"You know what we need?" Tabitha said, her dark eyes twinkling.

"What?"

"A sugar rush."

George grinned. "Are you thinking what I'm thinking?"

"Race you there!"

She sprinted off, and George followed. They screamed wildly, crashing into toppled stands and broken items, not stopping until they reached the kitchen. They opened the freezer and found—to their delight—that Strongarm didn't have time to save her Triple-dipple Ultra-deluxe Melty Creamy Creamer Rainbow Swizzle Milk Munch ice cream. The freezer held eight cartons. There was no way they could eat it all—but nothing could stop them from trying.

"TRIPLE-DIPPLE!" they both shouted, and they dug in.

The ice cream was even *better* than he remembered— but maybe it was because this time it tasted like victory.

George ate as much as he could and only stopped once he was on the verge of puking. Tabitha, too, groaned and clutched her stomach.

"I'm going to miss that the most!" she said, closing her eyes.

"I wonder if you can find this stuff on the Internet," George said. "I'd pay a lot of money for that ice cream."

"Really? You'd pay?" Tabitha said. "Hey—I'm *only joking!*" she added, catching the look on George's face.

Suddenly, the mansion thudded to a stop.

The Duke

George and Tabitha dashed out of the kitchen, leaped down the hall, and sprinted across corridors. They squealed as they slid all the way down the banister, from the third floor to the first—until they arrived in the foyer, just as the front doorknob was turning.

In walked the fanciest-looking man George had ever seen, with brown curls in perfect tendrils, a plump face with jibbling jowls, impressive muttonchops, and the air of being mollycoddled by hundreds of servants and attendants. But, George thought, perhaps it was just the outfit that was giving that impression, as the duke was wearing something that looked like it was from the six-teenth century: long white tights, a frilly blouse, poufy shorts, a dashing cape, and—to top it all off—a velvet hat with a feather in it.

George stepped forward, and the duke drew a fencing sword out of his holster, wielding it with wild eyes.

"Where iz he?! Ze one zey call ze Deanbugle?"

"Not here!" George said. "He jumped out the window! Put the sword down!"

"Calm down," the Duke of Valois said. "It iz blunt. For costume."

"Costume?"

"You zink I dress like zis on a daily basis?"

"Um . . . no?"

"Zat's right, no! I'm coming from ze most excellent costume party!" he clapped his hands, and two servants began to undress him. They removed his muttonchops—which were apparently stuck on—and his ruffled shirt before retreating with a bow. "My beautiful 'ome!" the Duke of Valois said, planting a big, wet, slobbery kiss on the banister.

George sat down on the step, and as he looked up, he saw the waitstaff headed down the stairs. George even saw Lionel and Hannah wave to him from the crowd.

"Do tell me 'ow you did it," the duke demanded.

And so George told them all about his experiences at Pilfer, with Tabitha jumping in to fill in the blanks and occasionally correct him—because old habits die hard.

The staff kept ooooohing and ahhhhhhing—and the duke listened very intently, particularly about the parts where Dean Dean Deanbugle was involved.

"Tell me again 'ow he jumped out ze window!" the duke said, giggling.

"We just told you three times," Tabitha said.

"But I want to 'ear it again!" he said petulantly.

"Okay, but after you tell *us* something," George said. "How did you get the planes to come so quickly?"

"I am rich," he said simply. "Ze problem was, I had no idea where zees mansion was. The world iz a very big place, you see. But once I knew ze location, I had ze resources."

"Very resourceful, sir!" one of the duke's servants said. "Very clever of you!"

"We need to talk about one thing," the Duke of Valois said. "What weel 'appen to all of you?"

The waitstaff all began to mumble among themselves. Some wanted to travel the world; others wanted to return home; others wanted to go back to school; and others still wanted to wait upon the honorable Duke of Valois, and he accepted them into his service with a giddy giggle.

"And what about ze children?" the duke said, smiling at them.

"Tabitha and I need to go home," George said.

"Then I weel arrange a plane in ze morning tomorrow! As for today? Go out on ze town! Explore! And enjoy zis one day vacation in France! You 'ave certainly earned it!"

The Same Old Different George

George had a *wonderful* day in France. The duke drove them around the countryside, and he and Tabitha walked around town. They peeked in the windows of stores, threw coins into a wishing fountain, and got to see a local historical house. But best of all, the duke bought them crepes, stuffed full of melted chocolate-hazelnut drizzle and fresh strawberries.

But the next morning, their mini-vacation was over and it was time to go home. George and Tabitha climbed into the duke's private jet. George had taken virtually nothing with him, since nothing he had at Pilfer actually belonged to him. But he did keep one thing that he knew he needed to deal with later.

Before George knew it, they were soaring. He pressed his nose against the window as the Duke of Valois's mansion became a pinprick in the distance before disappearing from his sight—and life—altogether.

And as the morning sun shone in through the plane, George leaned his head on Tabitha's shoulder and fell fast asleep.

When he woke up again, they were flying somewhere over some ocean. There was just blue sky and blue water as far as he could see in every direction.

"How long was I asleep?" George asked.

"Two hours, twenty-seven minutes, and forty-three seconds," Tabitha said. "I've been counting."

George gave her a look.

"Well, more or less."

George sighed and leaned back in his seat again. From his chair he watched the copilot eat an enormous ham sandwich.

"You know," said Tabitha. "I'm glad we did that."

"You are?"

"Yeah. I know I didn't feel the same way you did about the stealing, but it actually felt much better to be giving the mansion back to its proper owner than it felt to take things from people. I've been thinking . . . we should start our own thing. A club where we sneakily give people things."

"Like what?" George said.

"Like things they've lost. A service for returning lost or stolen items, if we ever come across any. For making people feel good. We have enough experience now to be able to run this in secret."

"The complete-opposite-of-crook-club club!" George said. "We'll have to work on the name a bit . . ." The plane made a sudden, turbulent jerk, and he gripped on to the seat for dear life.

"It'll be a good way to keep in touch," Tabitha suggested.

All too soon, the plane began to descend.

The pilot turned around. "You have your parachute strapped on?"

George nodded.

"Pull the lever on your shoulder to deploy the chute."

George turned to look at Tabitha, who was tearing up.

"Tabitha," he said, gearing up for what was sure to be a touching good-bye. "I am so gla—"

"Three-two-one GO!" the pilot shouted, pushing George out of the plane.

"AHHHHHHHHHHHHHHHHHHHHHHHHH!" George screamed as he free-fell toward solid ground, but then he remembered to deploy his parachute, and he began to glide.

It was peaceful, floating downward. He watched the

plane fly out of sight with a strange lump in his throat. He knew that he had done the right thing, but it didn't mean he wouldn't miss his best friend.

Don't forget about our new mission, he thought, and he instantly felt better.

He landed in a garden, crushing begonias under his bum. After he was shooed away by a cranky little man, George began marching toward home.

Of course, he didn't exactly know where home *was* from the cranky little man's garden, so he spent a good half hour getting completely lost. But, by the time the sun had set, he was finally walking into his house.

But he paused for a moment with his hand on the doorknob. He'd been so homesick for so long, and all he wanted to do now was fold up into his family's hugs. But it was also scary to be back home. The last time he was here, he was a completely different person. He'd changed so much in three months at Pilfer. What would they think of him now?

He opened the door.

Shoes clopped his way, and his mother rounded the corner.

Her jaw dropped when she saw him. "George!" his mother gasped. "JERRY! COME QUICK! KIDS! GEORGE IS HOME!"

261

Footsteps pounded across the house, and faces popped up from all around—his father came running from his office, Colby from upstairs, Gunther from the kitchen, Corman from the basement, and Rosie ran from the family room and tackled him round the middle.

After everyone had gotten at least five hugs in, they all settled in the family room. George's mom grabbed some cookies from the jar on the kitchen counter, arranged them on a platter, and served them to the family. And everyone kept firing questions at George so fast that his head was spinning.

"What's your favorite class?"

"What are your friends like?"

"How are your grades?"

"Do you like the food?"

"We've enjoyed your letters, George, honey."

At this, George furrowed his brow. "My *what*?"

"Your letters! The ones you've sent every week. Though your writing has been a bit . . . atrocious. I hope they're working on improving your writing skills?"

"Can I see one?" George asked.

"Of course! This one just arrived today—I wish you had warned us you were coming home, though—we have a lot of stuff on your side of the bedroom." His mother handed him a letter. It was written in chicken scratch that looked similar to his own, but he knew his own handwriting well enough to know that it wasn't his. He read the contents:

Dear Family,

I'm joying the very especial school. Thanks for sending me to Champeaux Institute for the Extra Ordinary Gifted and Talented Future Leaders of the World. And on scholarship, too!

This week, I'm meeting some of the a bassidors and ristorcats for supper and high tea. I love rumpets with preservatives—it's my most favoritist snack. Got to go meet some friends for homework—we have many essays to write about the constifusion of the United Steaks of America.

Love,

George Bucket

George smiled. This had Ballyrag written all over it. "Sorry, Mom," he said. "I was just in a rush."

"So tell us all about your school!" his dad said, biting into a cookie. "How much harder is it than public school?"

George thought about all the obstacle courses and the ridiculous tasks and the classes where he had to stand still for sixty minutes. "It was very difficult," he said. "And very different."

"Hey, isn't it a little early for winter break?" his big sister Colby asked. "It's only the first of November!"

"Oh, yeah, the school's no longer running anymore."

"No longer running?"

"George!" his mother said. "Y-you didn't get expelled or something, did you?"

His father spit out his last bit of cookie, mid-chew. *"Expelled?"*

"I didn't! I swear!"

His mother breathed a sigh of relief.

George thought of Tabitha, and how they'd worked together to do the right thing. How he did good, even when he was being taught to do the opposite, even when every adult had expected him to be a criminal.

George laughed. "I swear, I haven't been naughty. In fact," he added, beaming with pride, "I've actually been very, very good."

Doing Good

"Are we there yet?" George asked for the twentieth time in the last five minutes.

"No," his brother Derek said. "For the last time, we are *not there yet*."

George waited a moment. "Okay, how about now?"

"How about I turn this car around?" Derek grumbled.

George bounced in his seat; he could hardly wait. Ever since Derek arrived home from college for winter break, George had begged Derek to take him on a road trip. He could tell that his manipulation skills had gotten better at thief school because it only took Derek four days to cave—instead of his usual three weeks.

"Are we there yet?"

"Not. There. Yet." Derek rubbed his temples, like he had a really bad headache coming on. "What's so important to you about this trip? It's an awfully random town."

"There's just something I have to do, okay?"

"Something that involves . . . a teddy bear," Derek teased.

"Yes," George said, holding the teddy bear in his lap a little bit tighter. "It's important."

Derek shrugged. "You owe me big time, squirt."

"Thank you," George said. "And I promise to never touch your stuff again. Maybe."

Derek laughed.

At long last, the car slid to a stop in front of a white house, in a clustered neighborhood, in a valley beneath a hill.

"I'll be right back," George said, getting out of the car. He ran across the way, thankful that he had the foresight to have Derek park a few houses down.

For Derek's benefit, George pretended to ring the doorbell. But the second Derek looked down at his phone, George dove off the porch and crawled behind the bushes until he was out of Derek's line of sight. Then George went straight to the gutter, wrapped a sock around it, and began to use that to shimmy himself up the drainpipe. When—at last—he reached the roof, he rather ungracefully rolled himself onto the landing, crept over to the window, removed the screen, and yanked up on wood. The window slid open, just wide enough for George to wiggle inside.

There were noises coming from downstairs, and George knew he had to be extra quiet. So he tiptoed over to the crib and gently placed the stuffed bear beside the sleeping toddler.

He inched back to the window, put one foot outside, and when he turned around—the toddler was awake and blinking at him.

"Shhhhhh!" he said.

"Bear bear!" she hollered, jumping up and down in her crib. She was practically hyperventilating. "Bear bear! Bear bear!"

George squirmed the rest of himself through the window, and barely had time to shut it before her dad came bursting in.

"HONEY!" he hollered. "DID YOU FIND BEAR BEAR?"

"BEAR BEAR!" the toddler shrieked. "BEAR BEAR!"

Her mom came running into the room, and her parents celebrated the mysterious return of Bear Bear by taking turns tickling their toddler. Neither one of them even noticed George crouching outside the window, nose pressed up against the glass, a big, fat grin on his face.

To my many Partners-in-Crime:

Dean Dean Deanbugle once said that a good thief should never say thank you . . . but phooey to that!

First and foremost, thanks to my ~~family~~ crime ring: Mama "Mastermind" Mags, Dad "Bigcheese" Magaziner, and Michael "Mustacheman" Magaziner. I'll take you three in my getaway car every day!

To the Thieves of Team Dial—thanks for being my accomplices! Special thanks to Lauri "Headhoncho" Hornik and Namrata "Quickwit" Tripathi for all the cheerleading and support.

Rosanne "Safetynet" Lauer, thanks for catching all my mistakes. You're copyediting gold! Vanessa "Prowess" Robles, thank you for all your behind-the-scenes work and for keeping this book on track.

Thank you to my lovely cover designers: Cara "Craftmaster" Petrus, Maggie "Creativeflair" Olsen, and Dana "Artchamp" Li. And hugs to my wonderful interior designer: Nancy "Visionary" Leo-Kelly. You all made *Pilfer Academy* wickedly fun, inside and out!

To the Thieves of Marketing, Sales, Publicity, and School & Library: may you all be blessed with never-ending supplies of pasta

and Triple-dipple Ultra-deluxe Melty Creamy Creamer Rainbow
Swizzle Milk Munch Ice Cream.

Tara "Sweettalker" Shanahan, publicist extraordinaire! Thanks
for your enthusiasm, your savvy marketing ideas, and your
superhuman pitching skills. You are one smooth criminal!

Nancy "Suckerpunch" Conescu—you suckerpunched my first few
drafts in the very best way! Thanks for your editorial wisdom, for
helping me grow this idea from a seedling to a manuscript, for
laying the tracks in the beginning, and for shaping this book so
influentially.

Brianne "Sharkeyes" Johnson, my dearest darlingest crook! Thank
you for championing this book from the first time George laid
eyes on a T.rex riding a fighter plane. You know what? Thank you
just doesn't seem like enough. So instead, I shall appoint you the
Keeper of the Whirlyblerg (for all your dastardly whims).

Stacey "Wordwrencher" Friedberg, my clever editor and
Distinguished Thief of the Highest Honor. You are the Tabitha to
my George, the Strongarm to my Ballyrag, the eyebrows to my
Dean Dean Deanbugle. In other words: I truly could not have done
this without you. Every page, every paragraph, every sentence is
a shrine to your killer editorial instincts. Thank you—THANK
YOU—for believing in our thieves!

The Crowning Jewel of my thief career was the day I stole you all!